GOSCINNY AND UDERZO
PRESENT
An Asterix Adventure

THE
MANSIONS
OF
THE GODS

Written by RENÉ GOSCINNY *and Illustrated by* ALBERT UDERZO

Translated by Anthea Bell *and* Derek Hockridge

Orion
Children's Books

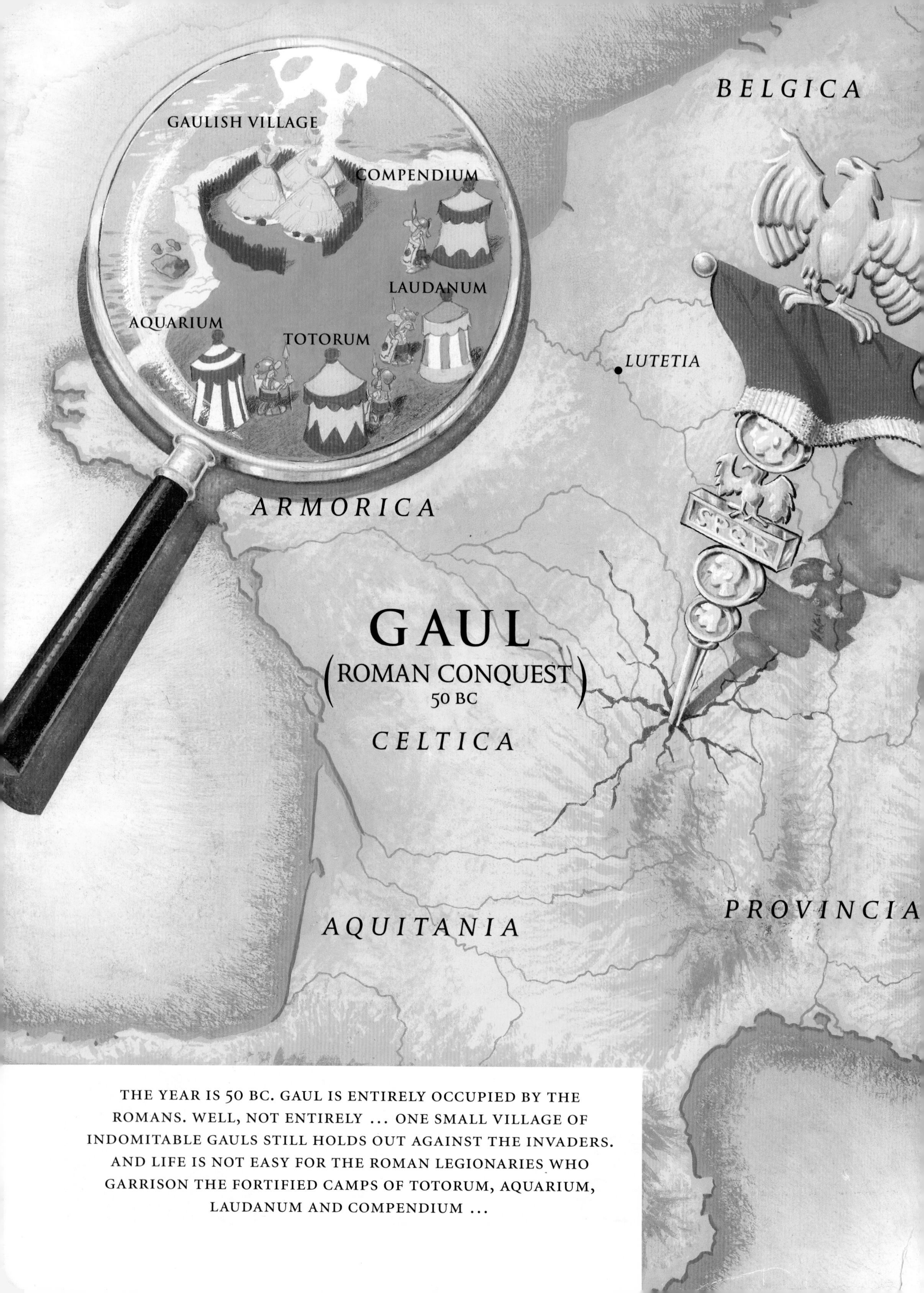
BELGICA
GAULISH VILLAGE
COMPENDIUM
LAUDANUM
AQUARIUM
TOTORUM
LUTETIA
ARMORICA
SPQR
GAUL
(ROMAN CONQUEST)
50 BC
CELTICA
PROVINCIA
AQUITANIA

THE YEAR IS 50 BC. GAUL IS ENTIRELY OCCUPIED BY THE ROMANS. WELL, NOT ENTIRELY ... ONE SMALL VILLAGE OF INDOMITABLE GAULS STILL HOLDS OUT AGAINST THE INVADERS. AND LIFE IS NOT EASY FOR THE ROMAN LEGIONARIES WHO GARRISON THE FORTIFIED CAMPS OF TOTORUM, AQUARIUM, LAUDANUM AND COMPENDIUM ...

ASTERIX, THE HERO OF THESE ADVENTURES. A SHREWD, CUNNING LITTLE WARRIOR, ALL PERILOUS MISSIONS ARE IMMEDIATELY ENTRUSTED TO HIM. ASTERIX GETS HIS SUPERHUMAN STRENGTH FROM THE MAGIC POTION BREWED BY THE DRUID GETAFIX . . .

OBELIX, ASTERIX'S INSEPARABLE FRIEND. A MENHIR DELIVERY MAN BY TRADE, ADDICTED TO WILD BOAR. OBELIX IS ALWAYS READY TO DROP EVERYTHING AND GO OFF ON A NEW ADVENTURE WITH ASTERIX – SO LONG AS THERE'S WILD BOAR TO EAT, AND PLENTY OF FIGHTING. HIS CONSTANT COMPANION IS DOGMATIX, THE ONLY KNOWN CANINE ECOLOGIST, WHO HOWLS WITH DESPAIR WHEN A TREE IS CUT DOWN.

GETAFIX, THE VENERABLE VILLAGE DRUID, GATHERS MISTLETOE AND BREWS MAGIC POTIONS. HIS SPECIALITY IS THE POTION WHICH GIVES THE DRINKER SUPERHUMAN STRENGTH. BUT GETAFIX ALSO HAS OTHER RECIPES UP HIS SLEEVE . . .

CACOFONIX, THE BARD. OPINION IS DIVIDED AS TO HIS MUSICAL GIFTS. CACOFONIX THINKS HE'S A GENIUS. EVERYONE ELSE THINKS HE'S UNSPEAKABLE. BUT SO LONG AS HE DOESN'T SPEAK, LET ALONE SING, EVERYBODY LIKES HIM . . .

FINALLY, VITALSTATISTIX, THE CHIEF OF THE TRIBE. MAJESTIC, BRAVE AND HOT-TEMPERED, THE OLD WARRIOR IS RESPECTED BY HIS MEN AND FEARED BY HIS ENEMIES. VITALSTATISTIX HIMSELF HAS ONLY ONE FEAR, HE IS AFRAID THE SKY MAY FALL ON HIS HEAD TOMORROW. BUT AS HE ALWAYS SAYS, TOMORROW NEVER COMES.

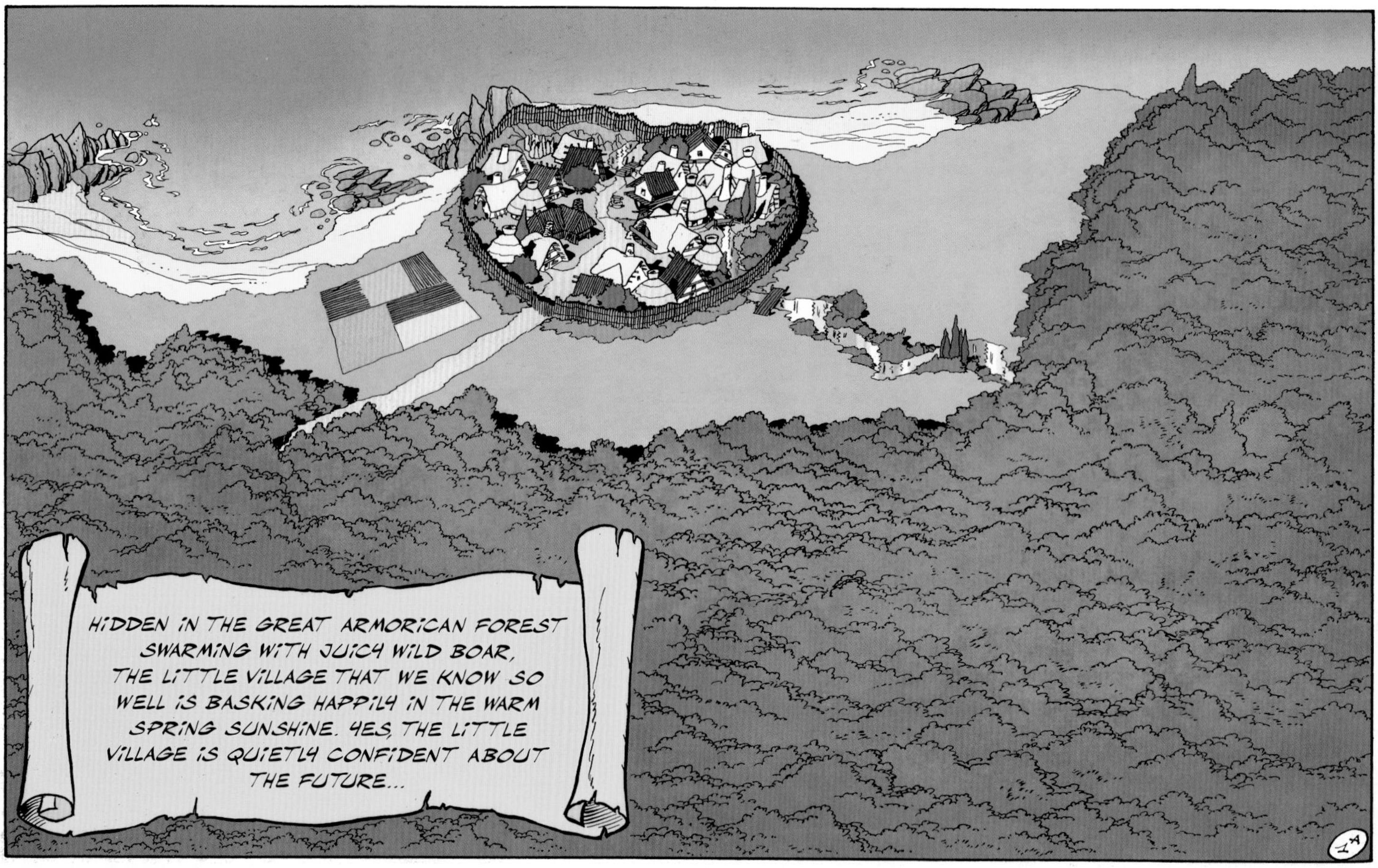
HIDDEN IN THE GREAT ARMORICAN FOREST SWARMING WITH JUICY WILD BOAR, THE LITTLE VILLAGE THAT WE KNOW SO WELL IS BASKING HAPPILY IN THE WARM SPRING SUNSHINE. YES, THE LITTLE VILLAGE IS QUIETLY CONFIDENT ABOUT THE FUTURE...
1A

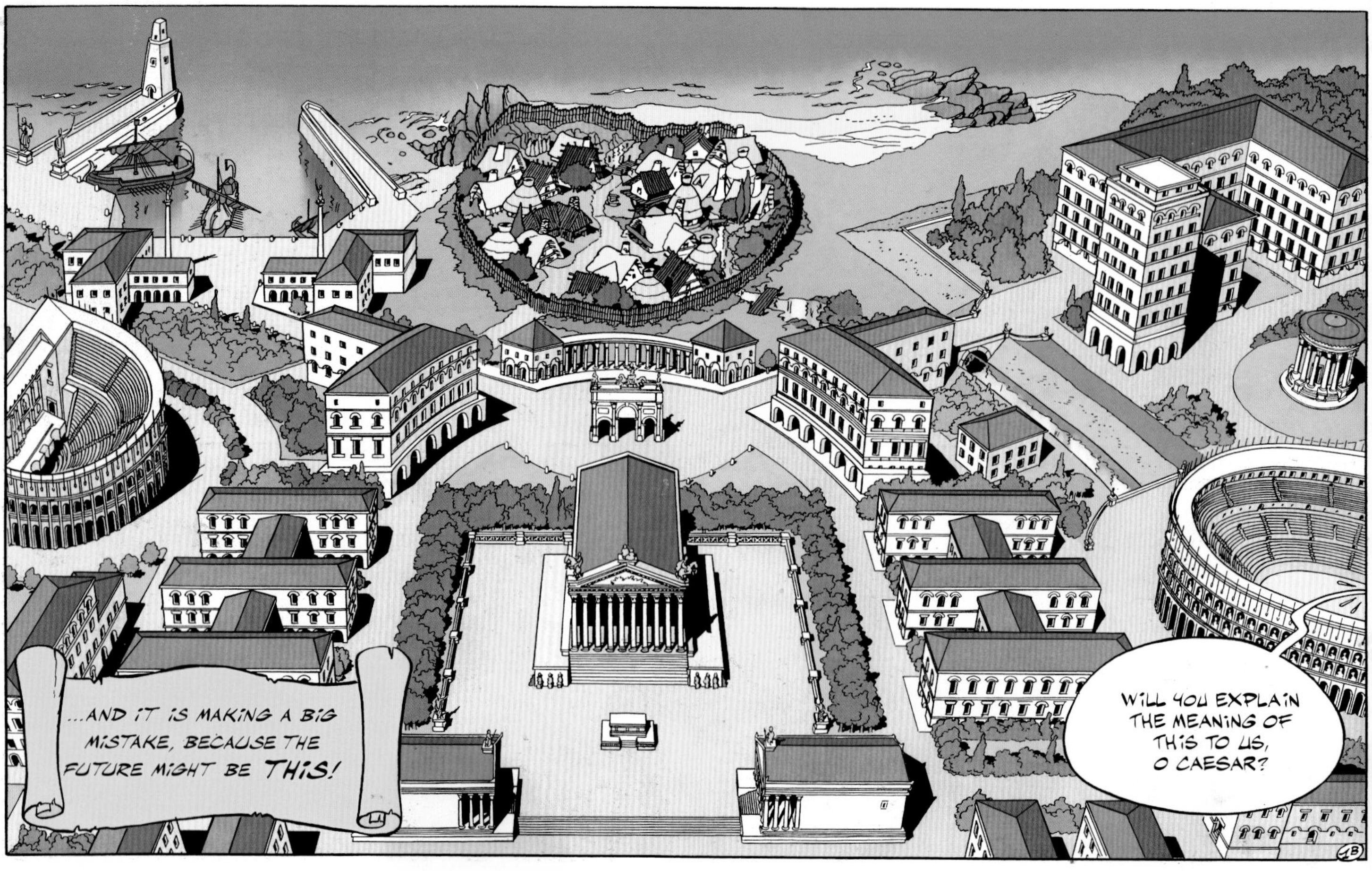
...AND IT IS MAKING A BIG MISTAKE, BECAUSE THE FUTURE MIGHT BE THIS!
WILL YOU EXPLAIN THE MEANING OF THIS TO US, O CAESAR?
1B

I WILL NOW GIVE YOU A BRIEF COMMENTARY. THE GAULS HAVING BEEN DEFEATED, THEIR CHIEF VERCINGETORIX LAID HIS ARMS AT THE FEET OF THE GLORIOUS GENERAL...

...WHO OCCUPIED ALL GAUL. ALL? NO! ONE SMALL VILLAGE INHABITED BY INDOMITABLE BARBARIANS DARED, AND STILL DARES, TO RESIST HIM!

WHO'S HE TALKING ABOUT?

HIMSELF. HE ALWAYS TALKS ABOUT HIMSELF IN THE THIRD PERSON.

HE'S GREAT!

ER... YOU!

WHO?

OH, HIM!

THESE GAULS, WITH THE AID OF A MAGIC POTION WHICH GIVES THEM SUPERHUMAN STRENGTH, AND PROTECTED BY A FOREST WHICH PROVIDES THEM WITH FOOD, REJECT THE ADVANTAGES OF ROMAN CIVILIZATION...

WHICH I HAVE DECIDED TO FORCE THEM TO ACCEPT! THE FOREST WILL BE DESTROYED TO MAKE WAY FOR A NATURAL PARK!

TCHAC!

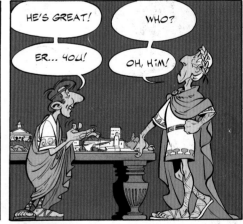

AND THEN BLOCKS OF FLATS FULL OF ROMAN TENANTS WILL SURROUND THE VILLAGE, WHICH WILL BECOME A MERE NATIVE RESERVATION. THESE GAULS MAY BE CRAZY *, BUT THEY'LL HAVE TO ADAPT TO OUR WAYS THEN!

* HENCE THE OLD GAULISH EXPRESSION 'A MENTAL RESERVATION'.

SO I HAVE CALLED IN ONE OF OUR MOST TALENTED YOUNG ARCHITECTS TO STUDY THIS PROJECT. I REFER TO SQUARONTHEHYPOTENUS...

NOT ONLY HAS SQUARONTHEHYPOTENUS BUILT MANY INSULAE*, SOME OF WHICH HAVE NOT FALLEN DOWN...

* BLOCKS OF FLATS

...HE IS ALSO THE INVENTOR OF THE DRIVE-IN AMPITHEATRE.

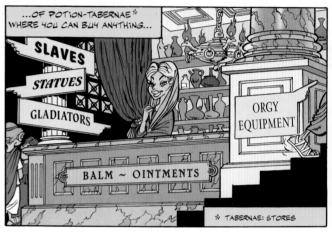

...OF POTION-TABERNAE* WHERE YOU CAN BUY ANYTHING...

SLAVES

STATUES

GLADIATORS

ORGY EQUIPMENT

BALM ~ OINTMENTS

* TABERNAE: STORES

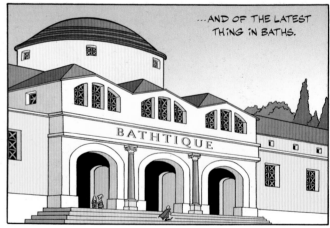

...AND OF THE LATEST THING IN BATHS.

BATHTIQUE

AND WHAT ARE YOU GOING TO CALL THIS NEW DEVELOPMENT WHICH IS TO CIVILIZE THE GAULS?

SQUARONTHEHYPOTENUS WANTED TO CALL IT ROME NEW TOWN, BUT THERE IS ONLY ONE ROME...

SO I HAVE DECIDED TO CALL IT 'THE MANSIONS OF THE GODS'... THAT WILL HELP TO PULL IN THE CUSTOMERS.

3

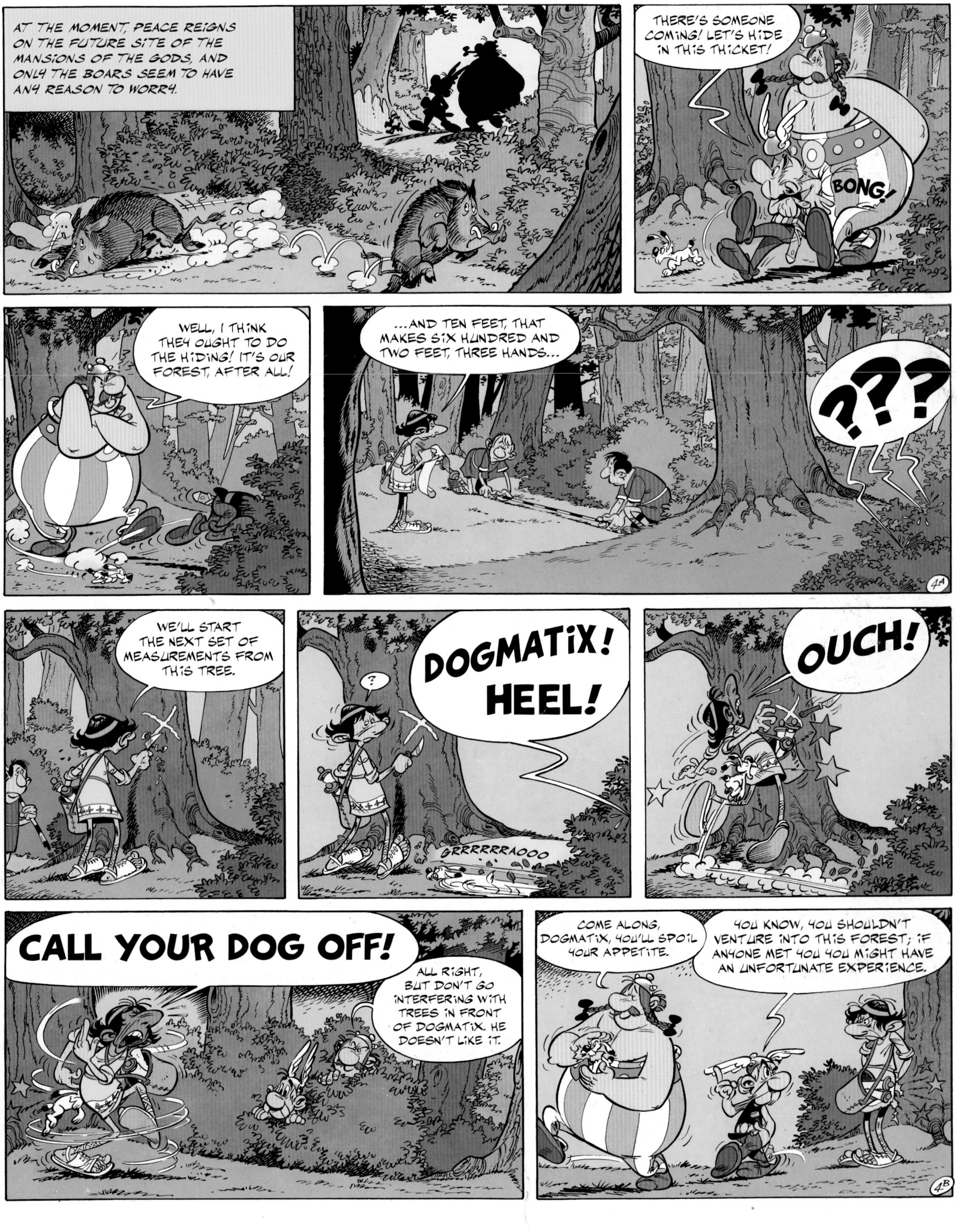
AT THE MOMENT, PEACE REIGNS ON THE FUTURE SITE OF THE MANSIONS OF THE GODS, AND ONLY THE BOARS SEEM TO HAVE ANY REASON TO WORRY.
THERE'S SOMEONE COMING! LET'S HIDE IN THIS THICKET!
BONG!
WELL, I THINK THEY OUGHT TO DO THE HIDING! IT'S OUR FOREST, AFTER ALL!
...AND TEN FEET, THAT MAKES SIX HUNDRED AND TWO FEET, THREE HANDS...
???
WE'LL START THE NEXT SET OF MEASUREMENTS FROM THIS TREE.
?
DOGMATIX! HEEL!
GRRRRRRAOOO
OUCH!
CALL YOUR DOG OFF!
ALL RIGHT, BUT DON'T GO INTERFERING WITH TREES IN FRONT OF DOGMATIX. HE DOESN'T LIKE IT.
COME ALONG, DOGMATIX, YOU'LL SPOIL YOUR APPETITE.
YOU KNOW, YOU SHOULDN'T VENTURE INTO THIS FOREST; IF ANYONE MET YOU YOU MIGHT HAVE AN UNFORTUNATE EXPERIENCE.

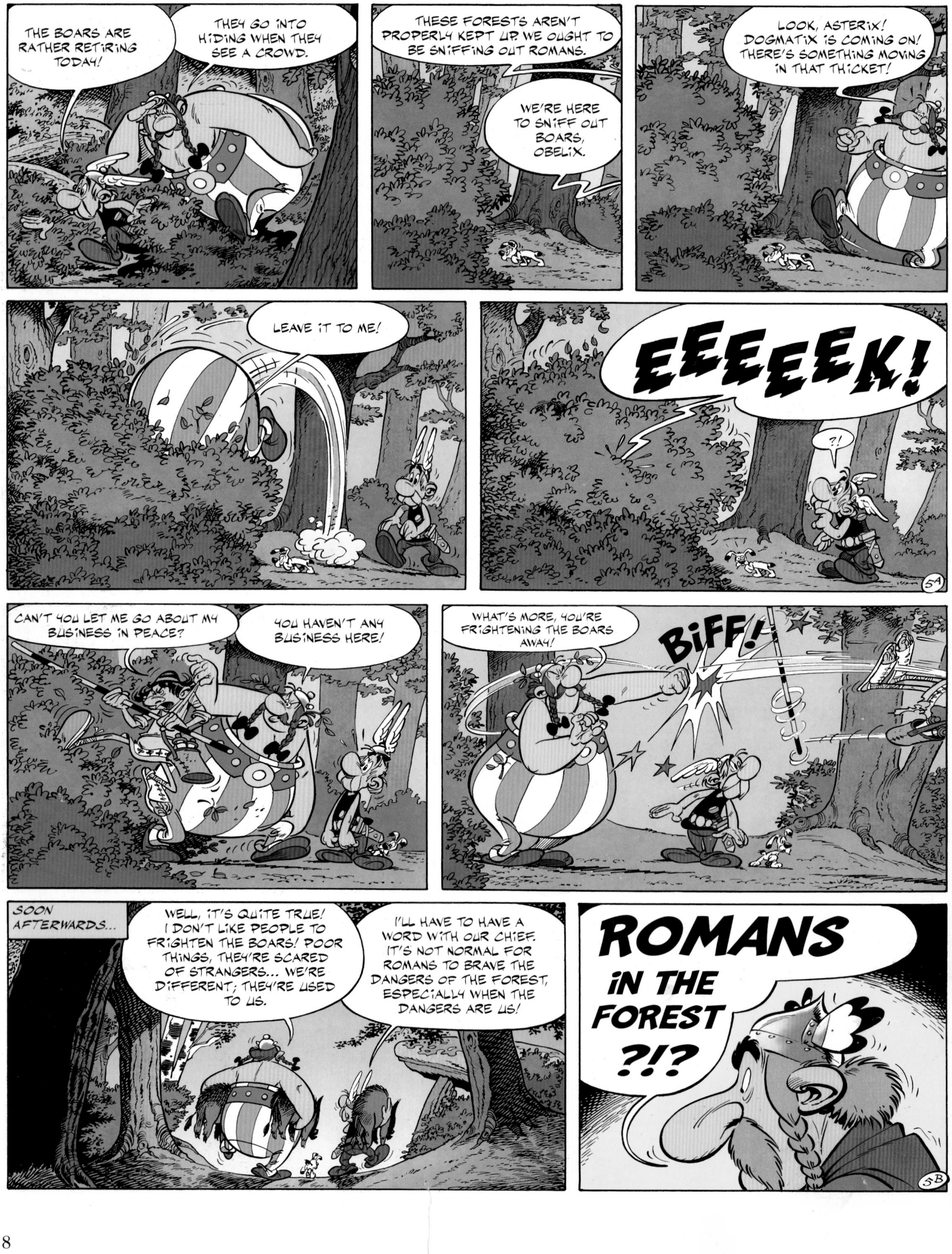

THE BOARS ARE RATHER RETIRING TODAY!
THEY GO INTO HIDING WHEN THEY SEE A CROWD.
THESE FORESTS AREN'T PROPERLY KEPT UP. WE OUGHT TO BE SNIFFING OUT ROMANS.
WE'RE HERE TO SNIFF OUT BOARS, OBELIX.
LOOK, ASTERIX! DOGMATIX IS COMING ON! THERE'S SOMETHING MOVING IN THAT THICKET!
LEAVE IT TO ME!
EEEEEEK!
?!
CAN'T YOU LET ME GO ABOUT MY BUSINESS IN PEACE?
YOU HAVEN'T ANY BUSINESS HERE!
WHAT'S MORE, YOU'RE FRIGHTENING THE BOARS AWAY!
BIFF!
SOON AFTERWARDS...
WELL, IT'S QUITE TRUE! I DON'T LIKE PEOPLE TO FRIGHTEN THE BOARS! POOR THINGS, THEY'RE SCARED OF STRANGERS... WE'RE DIFFERENT; THEY'RE USED TO US.
I'LL HAVE TO HAVE A WORD WITH OUR CHIEF. IT'S NOT NORMAL FOR ROMANS TO BRAVE THE DANGERS OF THE FOREST, ESPECIALLY WHEN THE DANGERS ARE US!
ROMANS IN THE FOREST ?!?

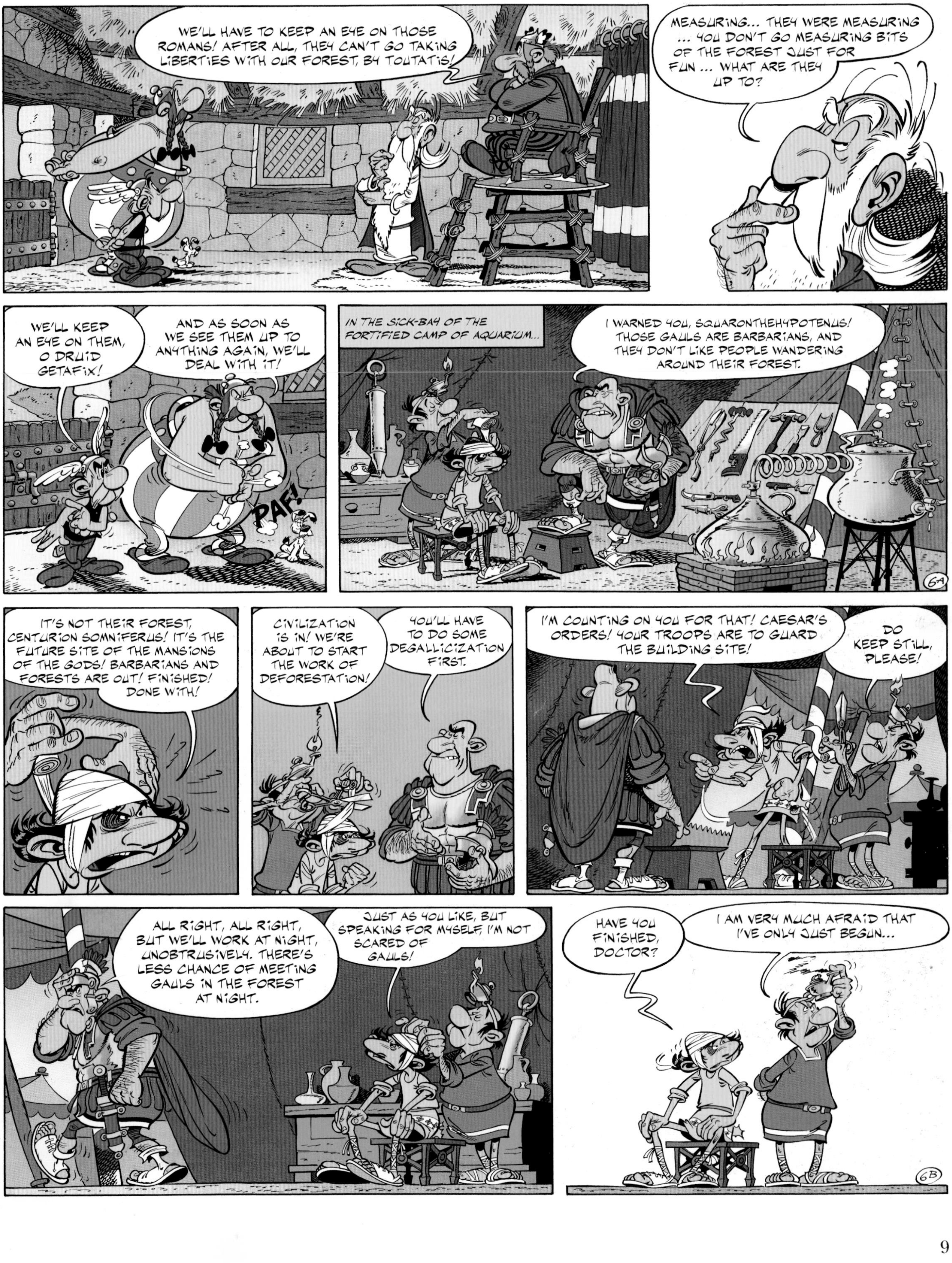
WE'LL HAVE TO KEEP AN EYE ON THOSE ROMANS! AFTER ALL, THEY CAN'T GO TAKING LIBERTIES WITH OUR FOREST, BY TOUTATIS!
MEASURING... THEY WERE MEASURING ... YOU DON'T GO MEASURING BITS OF THE FOREST JUST FOR FUN ... WHAT ARE THEY UP TO?
WE'LL KEEP AN EYE ON THEM, O DRUID GETAFIX!
AND AS SOON AS WE SEE THEM UP TO ANYTHING AGAIN, WE'LL DEAL WITH IT!
PAF!
IN THE SICK-BAY OF THE FORTIFIED CAMP OF AQUARIUM...
I WARNED YOU, SQUARONTHEHYPOTENUS! THOSE GAULS ARE BARBARIANS, AND THEY DON'T LIKE PEOPLE WANDERING AROUND THEIR FOREST.
IT'S NOT THEIR FOREST, CENTURION SOMNIFERUS! IT'S THE FUTURE SITE OF THE MANSIONS OF THE GODS! BARBARIANS AND FORESTS ARE OUT! FINISHED! DONE WITH!
CIVILIZATION IS IN! WE'RE ABOUT TO START THE WORK OF DEFORESTATION!
YOU'LL HAVE TO DO SOME DEGALLICIZATION FIRST.
I'M COUNTING ON YOU FOR THAT! CAESAR'S ORDERS! YOUR TROOPS ARE TO GUARD THE BUILDING SITE!
DO KEEP STILL, PLEASE!
ALL RIGHT, ALL RIGHT, BUT WE'LL WORK AT NIGHT, UNOBTRUSIVELY. THERE'S LESS CHANCE OF MEETING GAULS IN THE FOREST AT NIGHT.
JUST AS YOU LIKE, BUT SPEAKING FOR MYSELF, I'M NOT SCARED OF GAULS!
HAVE YOU FINISHED, DOCTOR?
I AM VERY MUCH AFRAID THAT I'VE ONLY JUST BEGUN...

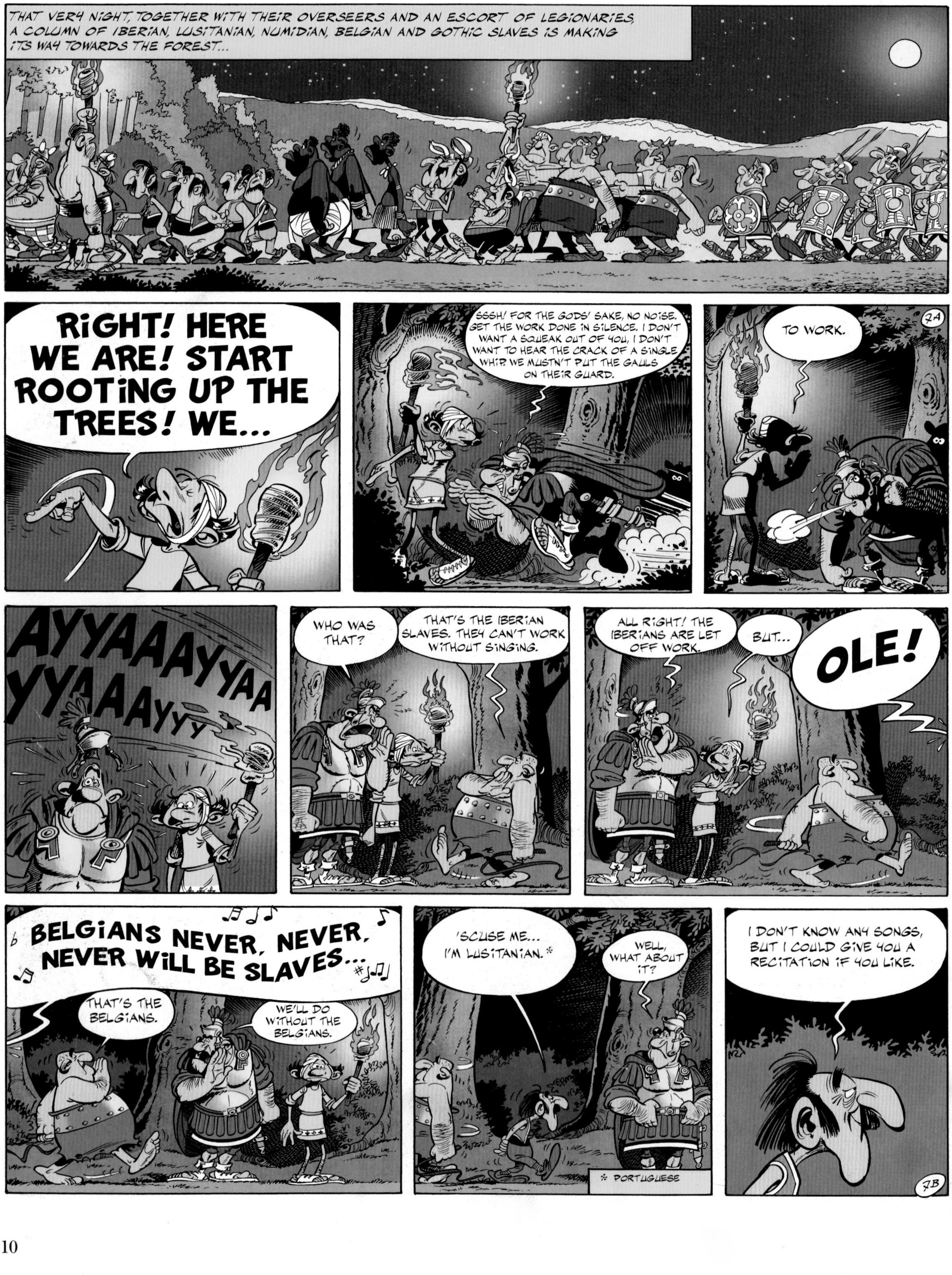

THAT VERY NIGHT, TOGETHER WITH THEIR OVERSEERS AND AN ESCORT OF LEGIONARIES, A COLUMN OF IBERIAN, LUSITANIAN, NUMIDIAN, BELGIAN AND GOTHIC SLAVES IS MAKING ITS WAY TOWARDS THE FOREST...
RIGHT! HERE WE ARE! START ROOTING UP THE TREES! WE...
SSSH! FOR THE GODS' SAKE, NO NOISE. GET THE WORK DONE IN SILENCE. I DON'T WANT A SQUEAK OUT OF YOU, I DON'T WANT TO HEAR THE CRACK OF A SINGLE WHIP. WE MUSTN'T PUT THE GAULS ON THEIR GUARD.
TO WORK.
AYYAAAAYYAA YYAAAAYYY
WHO WAS THAT?
THAT'S THE IBERIAN SLAVES. THEY CAN'T WORK WITHOUT SINGING.
ALL RIGHT! THE IBERIANS ARE LET OFF WORK.
BUT...
OLE!
BELGIANS NEVER, NEVER, NEVER WILL BE SLAVES...
THAT'S THE BELGIANS.
WE'LL DO WITHOUT THE BELGIANS.
'SCUSE ME... I'M LUSITANIAN.*
WELL, WHAT ABOUT IT?
* PORTUGUESE
I DON'T KNOW ANY SONGS, BUT I COULD GIVE YOU A RECITATION IF YOU LIKE.

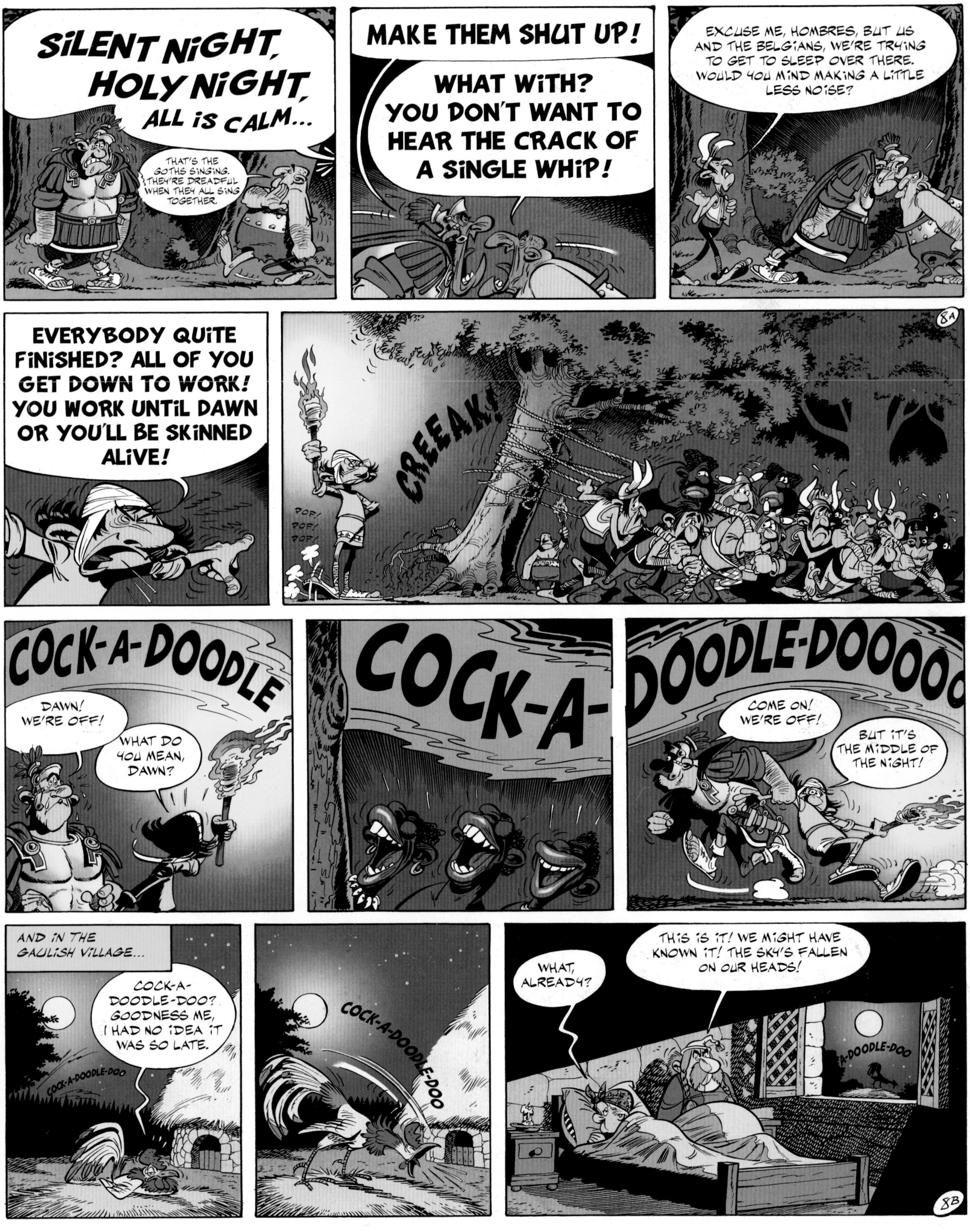
SILENT NIGHT, HOLY NIGHT, ALL IS CALM...
THAT'S THE GOTHS SINGING. THEY'RE DREADFUL WHEN THEY ALL SING TOGETHER.
MAKE THEM SHUT UP!
WHAT WITH? YOU DON'T WANT TO HEAR THE CRACK OF A SINGLE WHIP!
EXCUSE ME, HOMBRES, BUT US AND THE BELGIANS, WE'RE TRYING TO GET TO SLEEP OVER THERE. WOULD YOU MIND MAKING A LITTLE LESS NOISE?
EVERYBODY QUITE FINISHED? ALL OF YOU GET DOWN TO WORK! YOU WORK UNTIL DAWN OR YOU'LL BE SKINNED ALIVE!
CREEAK!
POP! POP! POP!
COCK-A-DOODLE
DAWN! WE'RE OFF!
WHAT DO YOU MEAN, DAWN?
COCK-A-
DOODLE-DOOOOO
COME ON! WE'RE OFF!
BUT IT'S THE MIDDLE OF THE NIGHT!
AND IN THE GAULISH VILLAGE...
COCK-A-DOODLE-DOO? GOODNESS ME, I HAD NO IDEA IT WAS SO LATE.
COCK-A-DOODLE-DOO
COCK-A-DOODLE-DOO
WHAT, ALREADY?
THIS IS IT! WE MIGHT HAVE KNOWN IT! THE SKY'S FALLEN ON OUR HEADS!
A-DOODLE-DOO

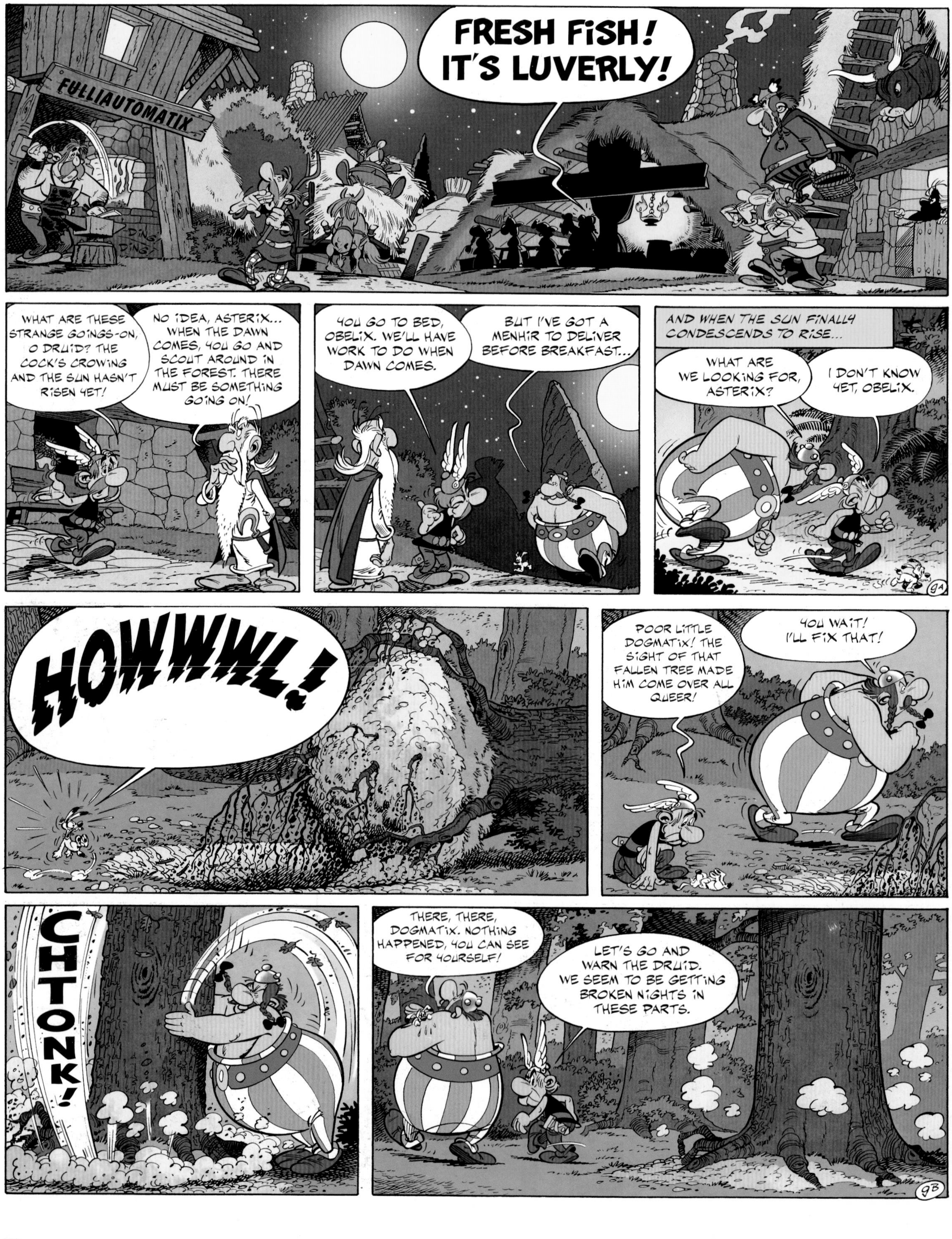
FULLIAUTOMATIX
FRESH FISH! IT'S LUVERLY!
DING DING
WHAT ARE THESE STRANGE GOINGS-ON, O DRUID? THE COCK'S CROWING AND THE SUN HASN'T RISEN YET!
NO IDEA, ASTERIX... WHEN THE DAWN COMES, YOU GO AND SCOUT AROUND IN THE FOREST. THERE MUST BE SOMETHING GOING ON!
YOU GO TO BED, OBELIX. WE'LL HAVE WORK TO DO WHEN DAWN COMES.
BUT I'VE GOT A MENHIR TO DELIVER BEFORE BREAKFAST...
AND WHEN THE SUN FINALLY CONDESCENDS TO RISE...
WHAT ARE WE LOOKING FOR, ASTERIX?
I DON'T KNOW YET, OBELIX.
9A
HOWWWL!
POOR LITTLE DOGMATIX! THE SIGHT OF THAT FALLEN TREE MADE HIM COME OVER ALL QUEER!
YOU WAIT! I'LL FIX THAT!
CHTONK!
THERE, THERE, DOGMATIX. NOTHING HAPPENED, YOU CAN SEE FOR YOURSELF!
LET'S GO AND WARN THE DRUID. WE SEEM TO BE GETTING BROKEN NIGHTS IN THESE PARTS.
9B

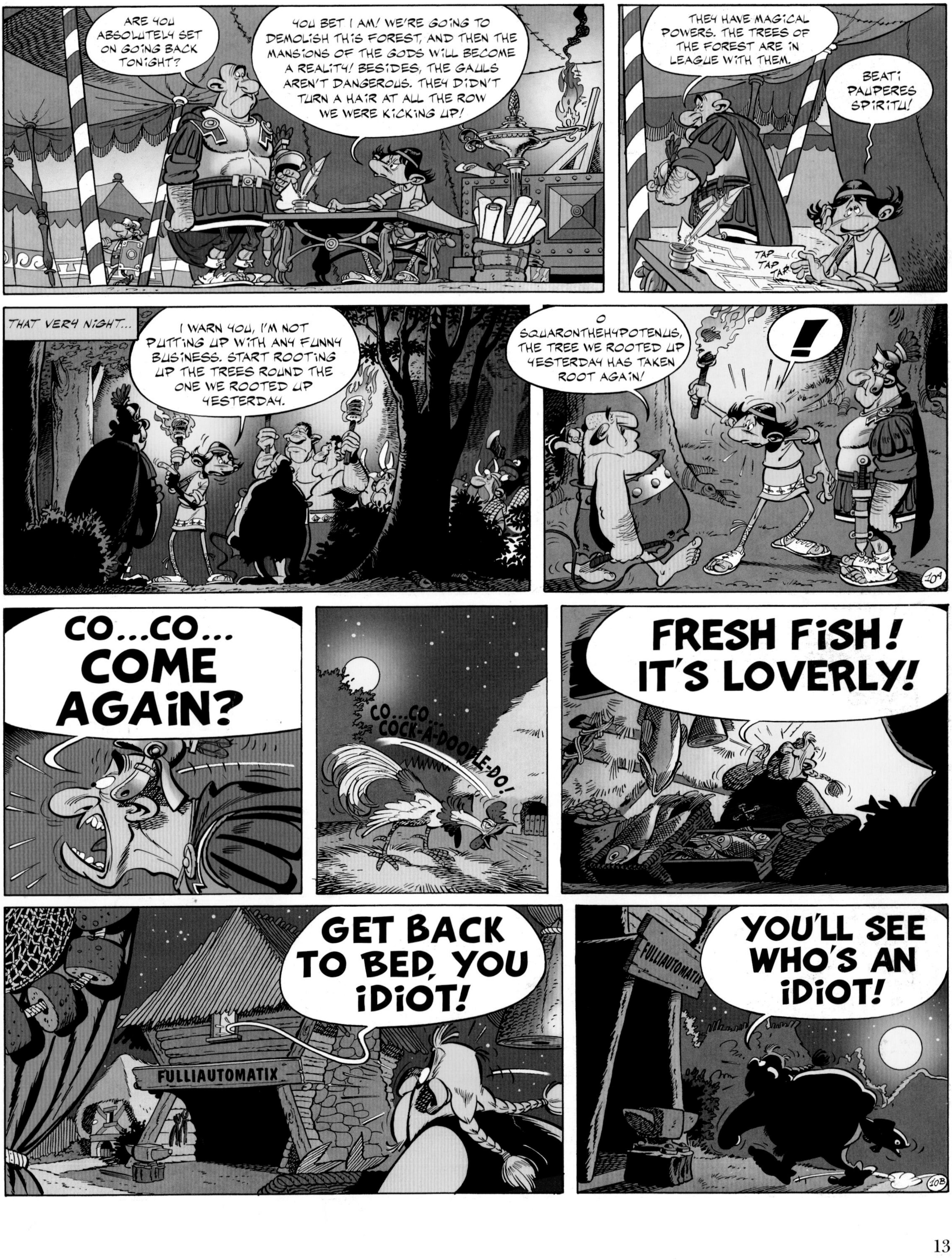
ARE YOU ABSOLUTELY SET ON GOING BACK TONIGHT?
YOU BET I AM! WE'RE GOING TO DEMOLISH THIS FOREST, AND THEN THE MANSIONS OF THE GODS WILL BECOME A REALITY! BESIDES, THE GAULS AREN'T DANGEROUS. THEY DIDN'T TURN A HAIR AT ALL THE ROW WE WERE KICKING UP!
THEY HAVE MAGICAL POWERS. THE TREES OF THE FOREST ARE IN LEAGUE WITH THEM.
BEATI PAUPERES SPIRITU!
TAP TAP TAP
THAT VERY NIGHT...
I WARN YOU, I'M NOT PUTTING UP WITH ANY FUNNY BUSINESS. START ROOTING UP THE TREES ROUND THE ONE WE ROOTED UP YESTERDAY.
O SQUARONTHEHYPOTENUS, THE TREE WE ROOTED UP YESTERDAY HAS TAKEN ROOT AGAIN!
!
CO...CO... COME AGAIN?
CO...CO... COCK-A-DOODLE-DO!
FRESH FISH! IT'S LOVERLY!
GET BACK TO BED, YOU IDIOT!
FULLIAUTOMATIX
YOU'LL SEE WHO'S AN IDIOT!
FULLIAUTOMATIX

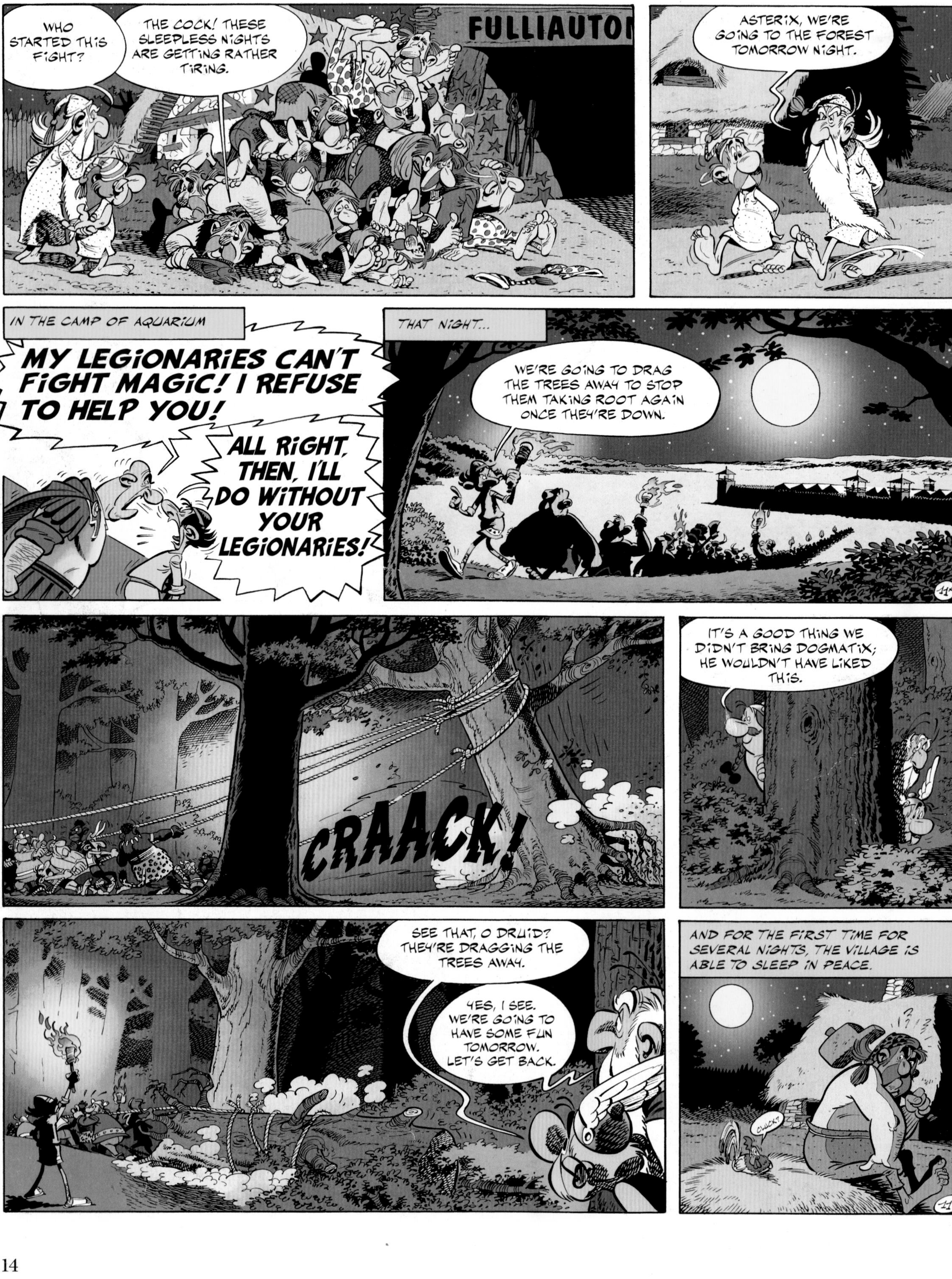
FULLIAUTO
WHO STARTED THIS FIGHT?
THE COCK! THESE SLEEPLESS NIGHTS ARE GETTING RATHER TIRING.
ASTERIX, WE'RE GOING TO THE FOREST TOMORROW NIGHT.
IN THE CAMP OF AQUARIUM
MY LEGIONARIES CAN'T FIGHT MAGIC! I REFUSE TO HELP YOU!
ALL RIGHT, THEN, I'LL DO WITHOUT YOUR LEGIONARIES!
THAT NIGHT...
WE'RE GOING TO DRAG THE TREES AWAY TO STOP THEM TAKING ROOT AGAIN ONCE THEY'RE DOWN.
CRAACK!
IT'S A GOOD THING WE DIDN'T BRING DOGMATIX; HE WOULDN'T HAVE LIKED THIS.
SEE THAT, O DRUID? THEY'RE DRAGGING THE TREES AWAY.
YES, I SEE. WE'RE GOING TO HAVE SOME FUN TOMORROW. LET'S GET BACK.
AND FOR THE FIRST TIME FOR SEVERAL NIGHTS, THE VILLAGE IS ABLE TO SLEEP IN PEACE.

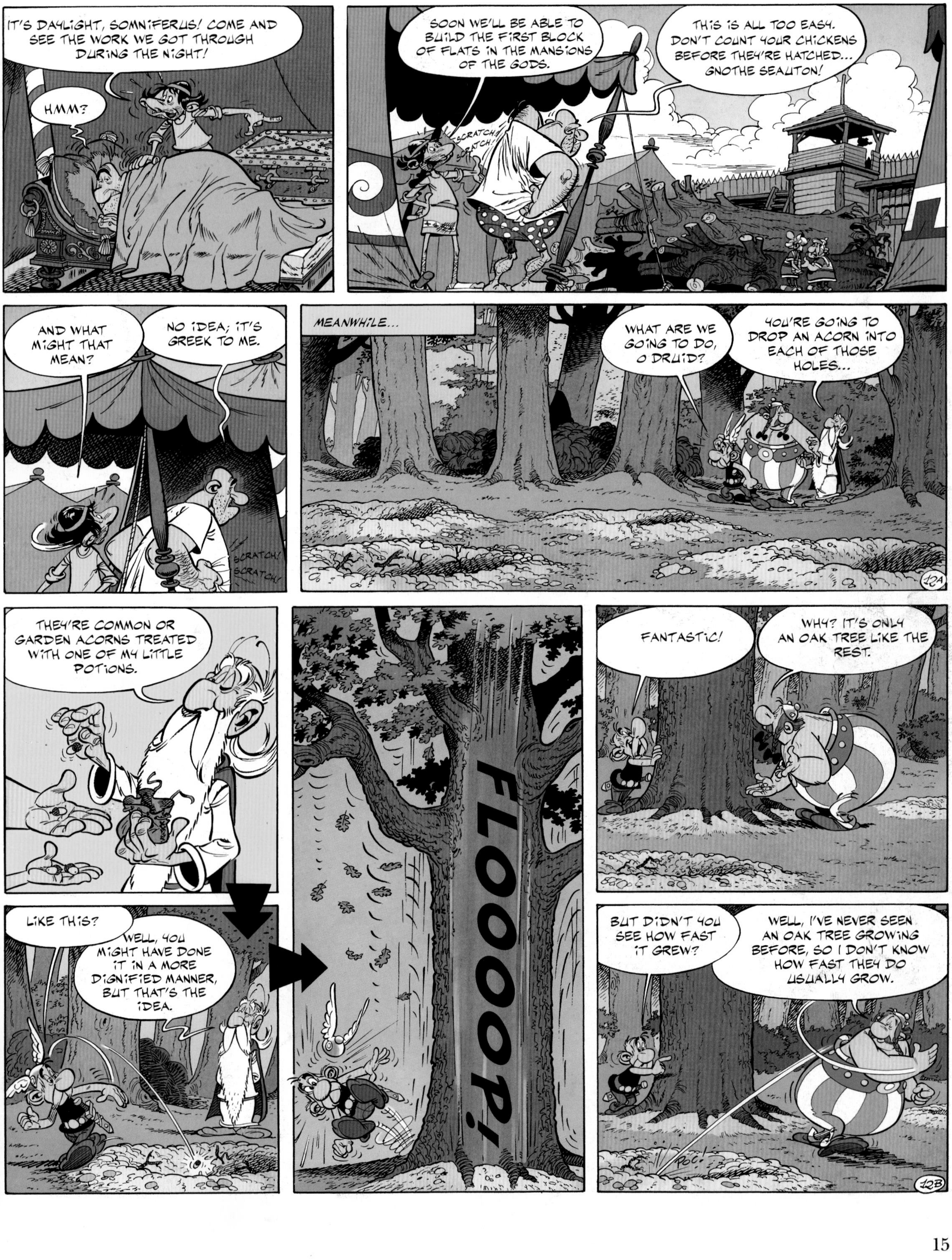

IT'S DAYLIGHT, SOMNIFERUS! COME AND SEE THE WORK WE GOT THROUGH DURING THE NIGHT!
HMM?
SOON WE'LL BE ABLE TO BUILD THE FIRST BLOCK OF FLATS IN THE MANSIONS OF THE GODS.
SCRATCH! SCRATCH!
THIS IS ALL TOO EASY. DON'T COUNT YOUR CHICKENS BEFORE THEY'RE HATCHED... GNOTHE SEAUTON!
AND WHAT MIGHT THAT MEAN?
NO IDEA; IT'S GREEK TO ME.
SCRATCH! SCRATCH!
MEANWHILE...
WHAT ARE WE GOING TO DO, O DRUID?
YOU'RE GOING TO DROP AN ACORN INTO EACH OF THOSE HOLES...
12A
THEY'RE COMMON OR GARDEN ACORNS TREATED WITH ONE OF MY LITTLE POTIONS.
LIKE THIS?
WELL, YOU MIGHT HAVE DONE IT IN A MORE DIGNIFIED MANNER, BUT THAT'S THE IDEA.
FLOOOOP!
FANTASTIC!
WHY? IT'S ONLY AN OAK TREE LIKE THE REST.
BUT DIDN'T YOU SEE HOW FAST IT GREW?
WELL, I'VE NEVER SEEN AN OAK TREE GROWING BEFORE, SO I DON'T KNOW HOW FAST THEY DO USUALLY GROW.
POC!
12B

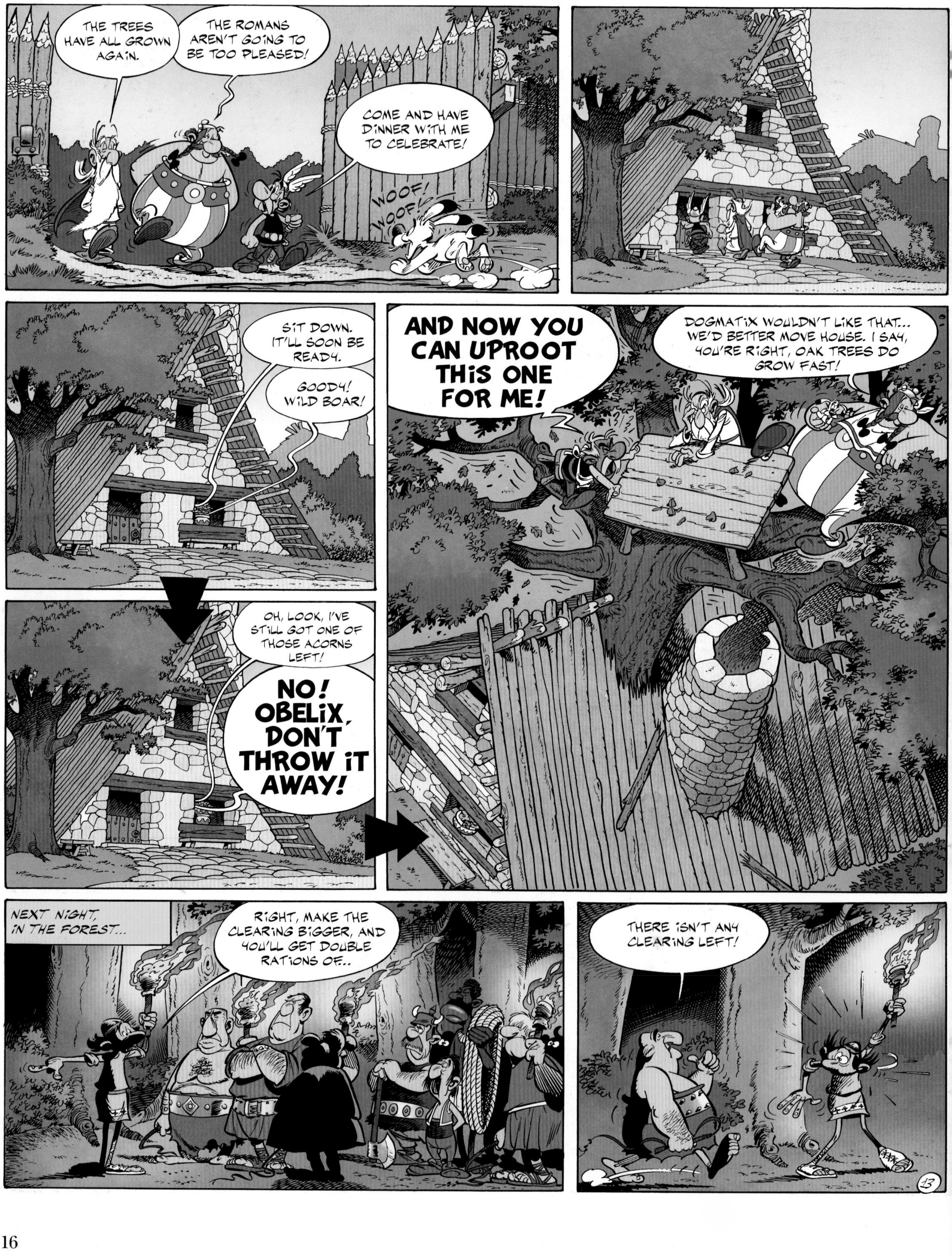
THE TREES HAVE ALL GROWN AGAIN.
THE ROMANS AREN'T GOING TO BE TOO PLEASED!
COME AND HAVE DINNER WITH ME TO CELEBRATE!
WOOF! WOOF!
SIT DOWN. IT'LL SOON BE READY.
GOODY! WILD BOAR!
OH, LOOK, I'VE STILL GOT ONE OF THOSE ACORNS LEFT!
NO! OBELIX, DON'T THROW IT AWAY!
AND NOW YOU CAN UPROOT THIS ONE FOR ME!
DOGMATIX WOULDN'T LIKE THAT... WE'D BETTER MOVE HOUSE. I SAY, YOU'RE RIGHT, OAK TREES DO GROW FAST!
NEXT NIGHT, IN THE FOREST...
RIGHT, MAKE THE CLEARING BIGGER, AND YOU'LL GET DOUBLE RATIONS OF..
THERE ISN'T ANY CLEARING LEFT!
13

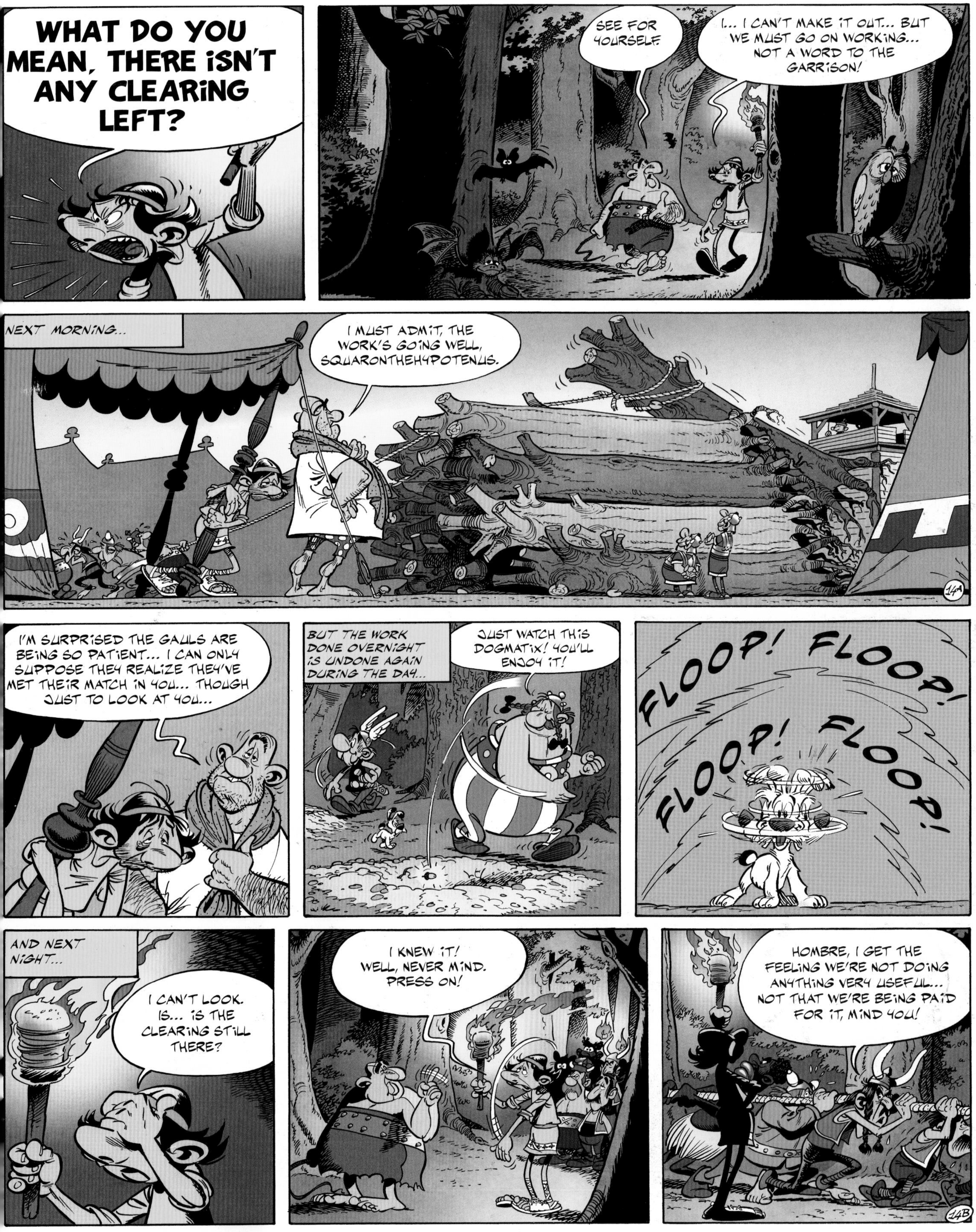
WHAT DO YOU MEAN, THERE ISN'T ANY CLEARING LEFT?
SEE FOR YOURSELF.
I... I CAN'T MAKE IT OUT... BUT WE MUST GO ON WORKING... NOT A WORD TO THE GARRISON!
NEXT MORNING...
I MUST ADMIT, THE WORK'S GOING WELL, SQUARONTHEHYPOTENUS.
14A
I'M SURPRISED THE GAULS ARE BEING SO PATIENT... I CAN ONLY SUPPOSE THEY REALIZE THEY'VE MET THEIR MATCH IN YOU... THOUGH JUST TO LOOK AT YOU...
BUT THE WORK DONE OVERNIGHT IS UNDONE AGAIN DURING THE DAY...
JUST WATCH THIS DOGMATIX! YOU'LL ENJOY IT!
FLOOP! FLOOP! FLOOP! FLOOP!
AND NEXT NIGHT...
I CAN'T LOOK. IS... IS THE CLEARING STILL THERE?
I KNEW IT! WELL, NEVER MIND. PRESS ON!
HOMBRE, I GET THE FEELING WE'RE NOT DOING ANYTHING VERY USEFUL... NOT THAT WE'RE BEING PAID FOR IT, MIND YOU!
14B

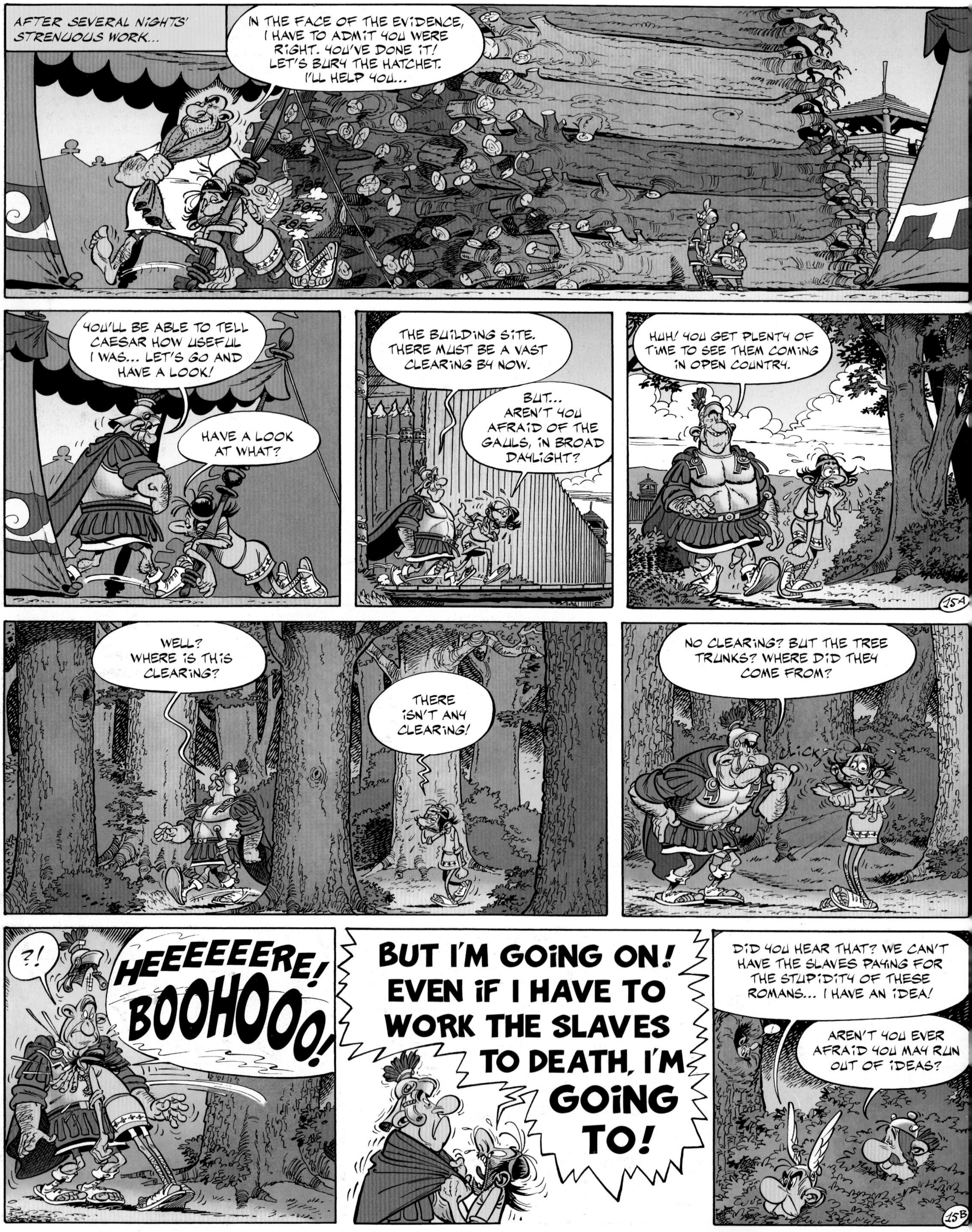
AFTER SEVERAL NIGHTS' STRENUOUS WORK...
IN THE FACE OF THE EVIDENCE, I HAVE TO ADMIT YOU WERE RIGHT. YOU'VE DONE IT! LET'S BURY THE HATCHET. I'LL HELP YOU...
YOU'LL BE ABLE TO TELL CAESAR HOW USEFUL I WAS... LET'S GO AND HAVE A LOOK!
HAVE A LOOK AT WHAT?
THE BUILDING SITE. THERE MUST BE A VAST CLEARING BY NOW.
BUT... AREN'T YOU AFRAID OF THE GAULS, IN BROAD DAYLIGHT?
HUH! YOU GET PLENTY OF TIME TO SEE THEM COMING IN OPEN COUNTRY.
WELL? WHERE IS THIS CLEARING?
THERE ISN'T ANY CLEARING!
NO CLEARING? BUT THE TREE TRUNKS? WHERE DID THEY COME FROM?
CLICK
?!
HEEEEEEERE! BOOHOOO!
BUT I'M GOING ON! EVEN IF I HAVE TO WORK THE SLAVES TO DEATH, I'M GOING TO!
DID YOU HEAR THAT? WE CAN'T HAVE THE SLAVES PAYING FOR THE STUPIDITY OF THESE ROMANS... I HAVE AN IDEA!
AREN'T YOU EVER AFRAID YOU MAY RUN OUT OF IDEAS?

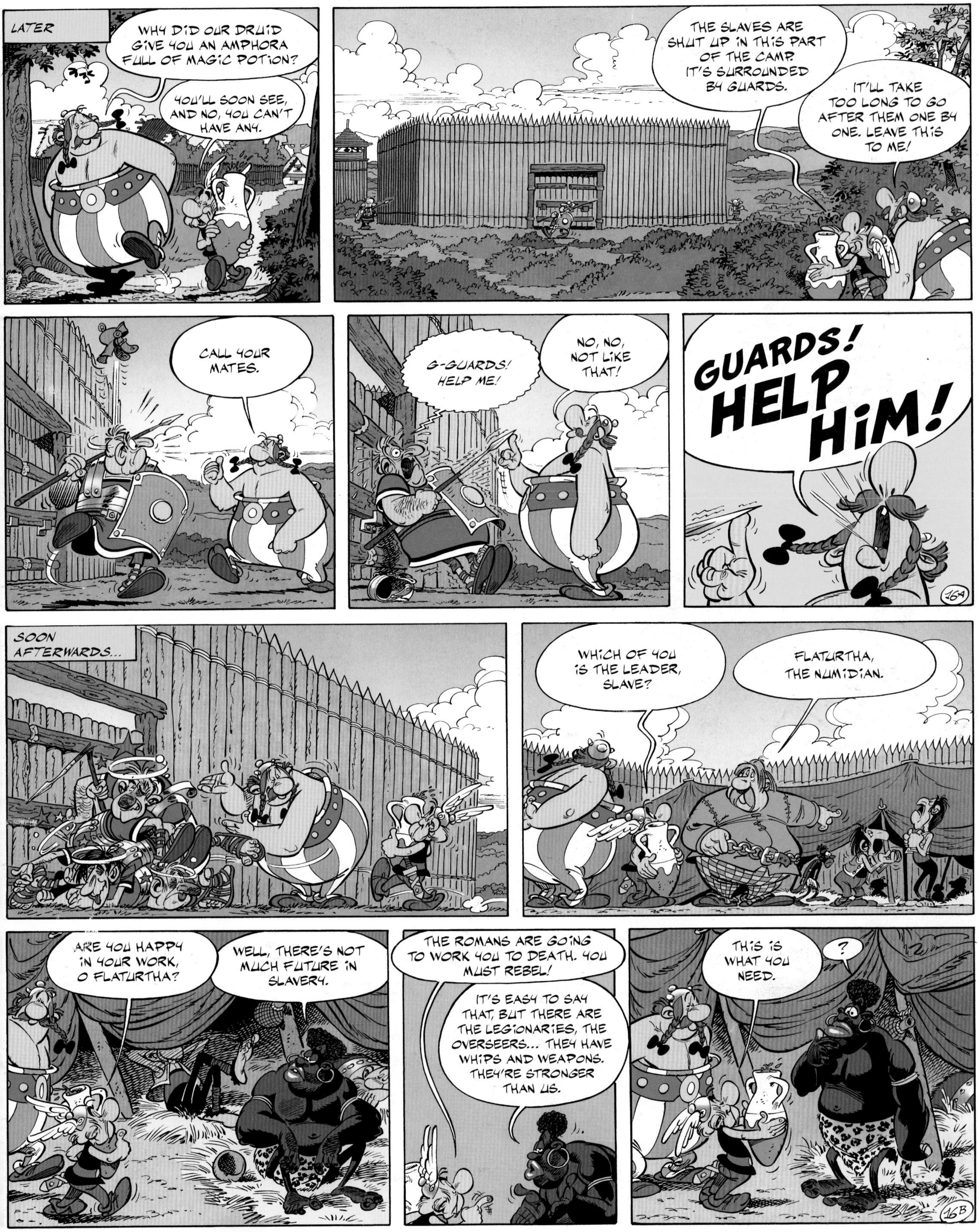
LATER
WHY DID OUR DRUID GIVE YOU AN AMPHORA FULL OF MAGIC POTION?
YOU'LL SOON SEE, AND NO, YOU CAN'T HAVE ANY.
THE SLAVES ARE SHUT UP IN THIS PART OF THE CAMP. IT'S SURROUNDED BY GUARDS.
IT'LL TAKE TOO LONG TO GO AFTER THEM ONE BY ONE. LEAVE THIS TO ME!
CALL YOUR MATES.
G-GUARDS! HELP ME!
NO, NO, NOT LIKE THAT!
GUARDS! HELP HIM!
SOON AFTERWARDS...
WHICH OF YOU IS THE LEADER, SLAVE?
FLATURTHA, THE NUMIDIAN.
ARE YOU HAPPY IN YOUR WORK, O FLATURTHA?
WELL, THERE'S NOT MUCH FUTURE IN SLAVERY.
THE ROMANS ARE GOING TO WORK YOU TO DEATH. YOU MUST REBEL!
IT'S EASY TO SAY THAT, BUT THERE ARE THE LEGIONARIES, THE OVERSEERS... THEY HAVE WHIPS AND WEAPONS. THEY'RE STRONGER THAN US.
THIS IS WHAT YOU NEED.
?

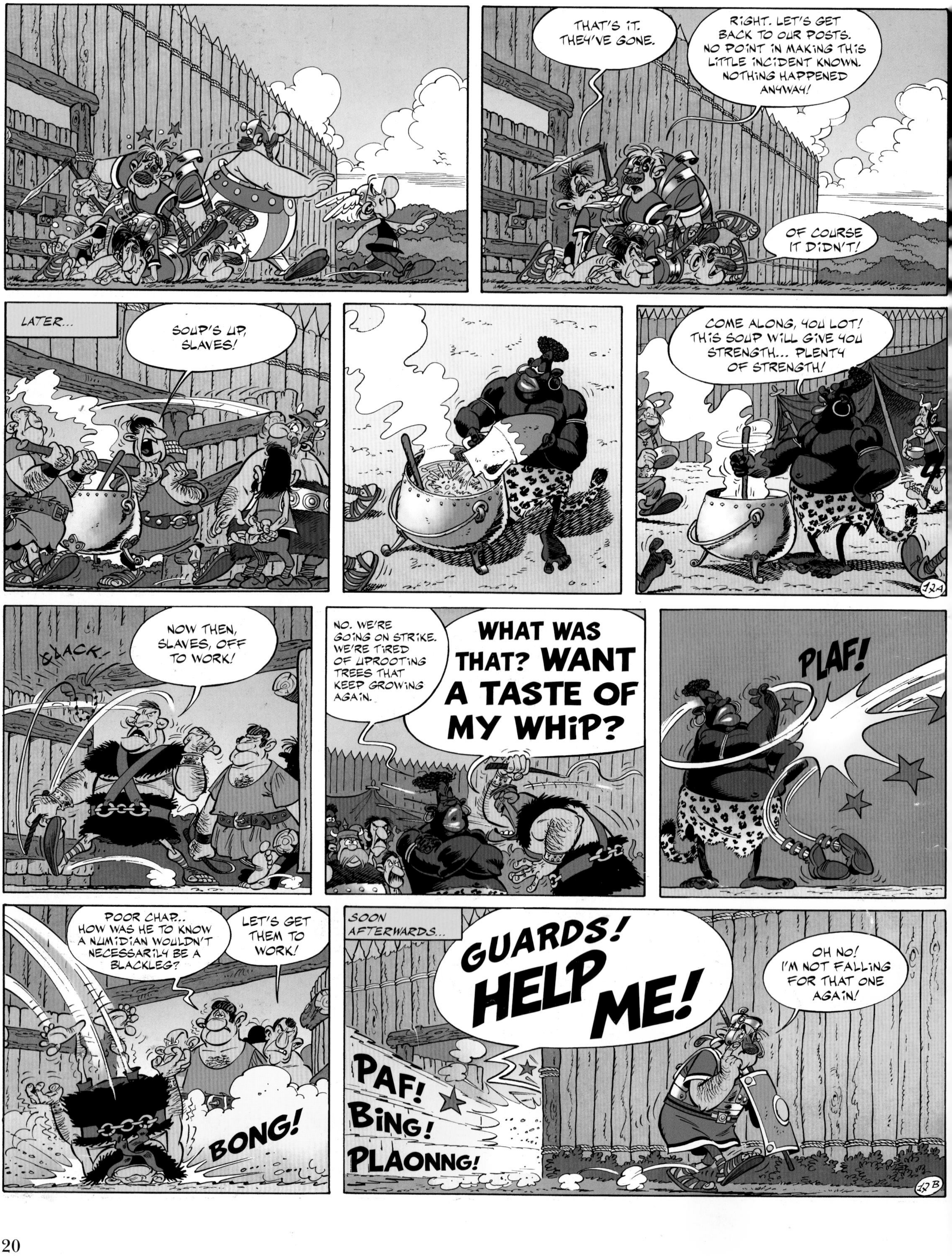

THAT'S IT. THEY'VE GONE.
RIGHT. LET'S GET BACK TO OUR POSTS. NO POINT IN MAKING THIS LITTLE INCIDENT KNOWN. NOTHING HAPPENED ANYWAY!
OF COURSE IT DIDN'T!
LATER...
SOUP'S UP, SLAVES!
COME ALONG, YOU LOT! THIS SOUP WILL GIVE YOU STRENGTH... PLENTY OF STRENGTH!
CLACK!
NOW THEN, SLAVES, OFF TO WORK!
NO. WE'RE GOING ON STRIKE. WE'RE TIRED OF UPROOTING TREES THAT KEEP GROWING AGAIN.
WHAT WAS THAT? WANT A TASTE OF MY WHIP?
PLAF!
POOR CHAP.. HOW WAS HE TO KNOW A NUMIDIAN WOULDN'T NECESSARILY BE A BLACKLEG?
LET'S GET THEM TO WORK!
BONG!
SOON AFTERWARDS...
GUARDS! HELP ME!
OH NO! I'M NOT FALLING FOR THAT ONE AGAIN!
PAF!
BING!
PLAONNG!

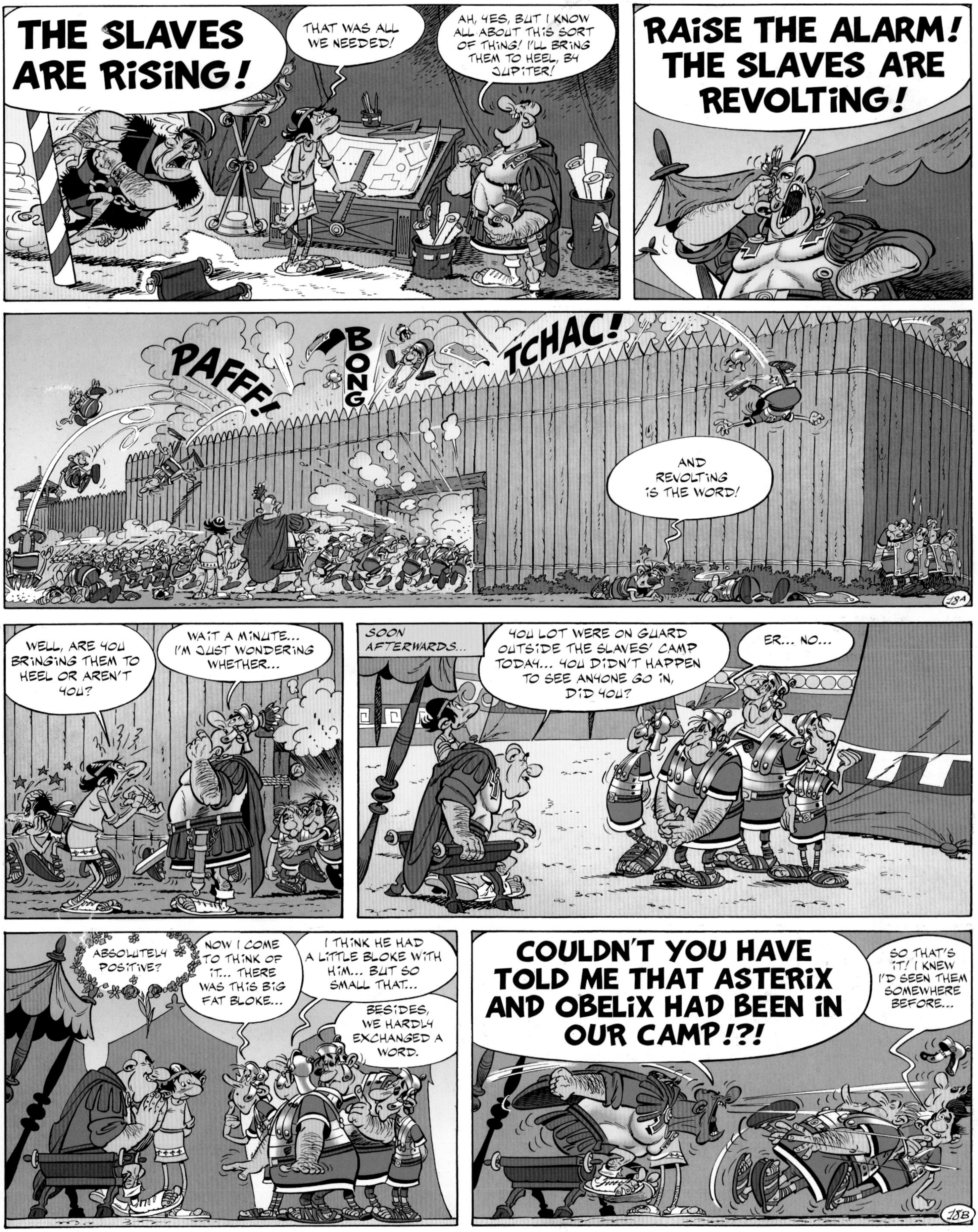
THE SLAVES ARE RISING!
THAT WAS ALL WE NEEDED!
AH, YES, BUT I KNOW ALL ABOUT THIS SORT OF THING! I'LL BRING THEM TO HEEL, BY JUPITER!
RAISE THE ALARM! THE SLAVES ARE REVOLTING!
PAFFF!
BONG
TCHAC!
AND REVOLTING IS THE WORD!
WELL, ARE YOU BRINGING THEM TO HEEL OR AREN'T YOU?
WAIT A MINUTE... I'M JUST WONDERING WHETHER...
SOON AFTERWARDS...
YOU LOT WERE ON GUARD OUTSIDE THE SLAVES' CAMP TODAY... YOU DIDN'T HAPPEN TO SEE ANYONE GO IN, DID YOU?
ER... NO...
ABSOLUTELY POSITIVE?
NOW I COME TO THINK OF IT... THERE WAS THIS BIG FAT BLOKE...
I THINK HE HAD A LITTLE BLOKE WITH HIM... BUT SO SMALL THAT...
BESIDES, WE HARDLY EXCHANGED A WORD.
COULDN'T YOU HAVE TOLD ME THAT ASTERIX AND OBELIX HAD BEEN IN OUR CAMP!?!
SO THAT'S IT! I KNEW I'D SEEN THEM SOMEWHERE BEFORE...

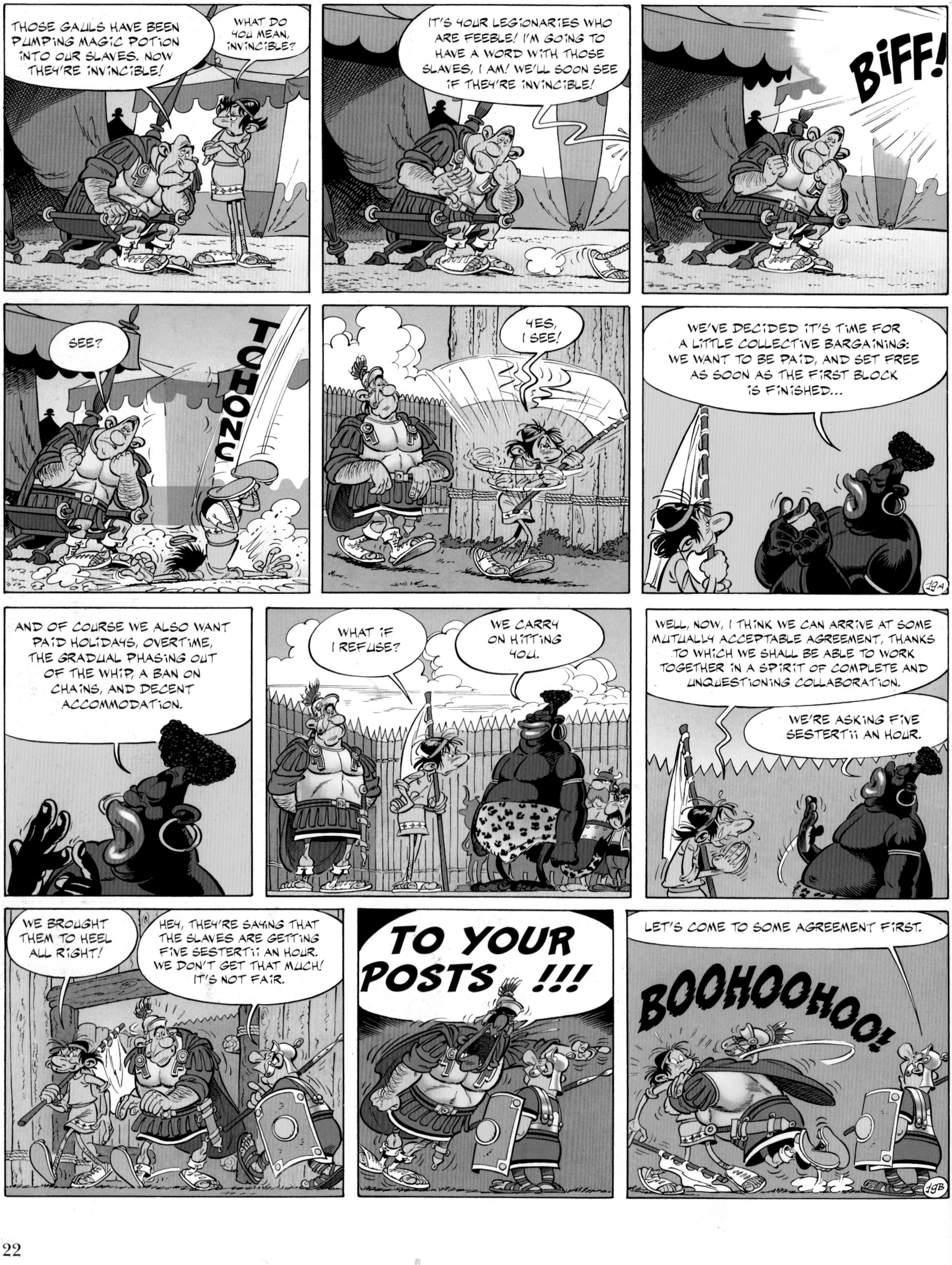
THOSE GAULS HAVE BEEN PUMPING MAGIC POTION INTO OUR SLAVES. NOW THEY'RE INVINCIBLE!
WHAT DO YOU MEAN, INVINCIBLE?
IT'S YOUR LEGIONARIES WHO ARE FEEBLE! I'M GOING TO HAVE A WORD WITH THOSE SLAVES, I AM! WE'LL SOON SEE IF THEY'RE INVINCIBLE!
BIFF!
SEE?
TCHONC
YES, I SEE!
WE'VE DECIDED IT'S TIME FOR A LITTLE COLLECTIVE BARGAINING: WE WANT TO BE PAID, AND SET FREE AS SOON AS THE FIRST BLOCK IS FINISHED...
AND OF COURSE WE ALSO WANT PAID HOLIDAYS, OVERTIME, THE GRADUAL PHASING OUT OF THE WHIP, A BAN ON CHAINS, AND DECENT ACCOMMODATION.
WHAT IF I REFUSE?
WE CARRY ON HITTING YOU.
WELL, NOW, I THINK WE CAN ARRIVE AT SOME MUTUALLY ACCEPTABLE AGREEMENT, THANKS TO WHICH WE SHALL BE ABLE TO WORK TOGETHER IN A SPIRIT OF COMPLETE AND UNQUESTIONING COLLABORATION.
WE'RE ASKING FIVE SESTERTII AN HOUR.
WE BROUGHT THEM TO HEEL ALL RIGHT!
HEY, THEY'RE SAYING THAT THE SLAVES ARE GETTING FIVE SESTERTII AN HOUR. WE DON'T GET THAT MUCH! IT'S NOT FAIR.
TO YOUR POSTS !!!
LET'S COME TO SOME AGREEMENT FIRST.
BOOHOOHOO!

WHILE SOMNIFERUS IS DEALING WITH HIS OWN LITTLE PROBLEMS, WORK HAS BEGUN AGAIN ON THE BUILDING SITE, NOW THAT THE AGREEMENT AND THE MAGIC POTION HAVE PROVED EFFECTIVE...

ALLEZ...

OOOP!

CRACK!

IT'S UNHEARD-OF! THE SLAVES HAVE BEEN WORKING BETTER SINCE WE STARTED PAYING THEM!

YES, IT MEANS MORE INITIAL OUTLAY, BUT BIGGER PROFITS!

AND THINK OF THE SAVING ON WHIPS!

I DON'T UNDERSTAND, ASTERIX! I THOUGHT THEY WERE GOING TO REBEL AGAINST THE ROMANS AND STOP WORK...

EEEK! THIS TREE'S MOVING!

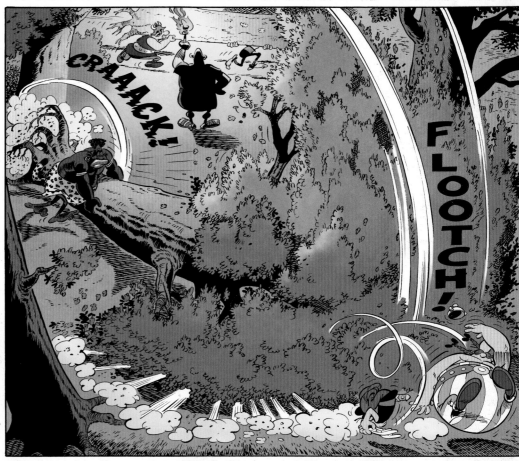

CRAAACK!

FLOOTCH!

FLATURTHA! WHY ARE YOU PULLING UP THESE TREES?

NO VISITORS ON THE BUILDING SITE. PUSH OFF!

LOOK HERE, NUMIDIAN...

OVERSEERS! NO SLACKING! I FEEL TIRED AND HUNGRY. I'D LIKE A QUICK WHIP!

20

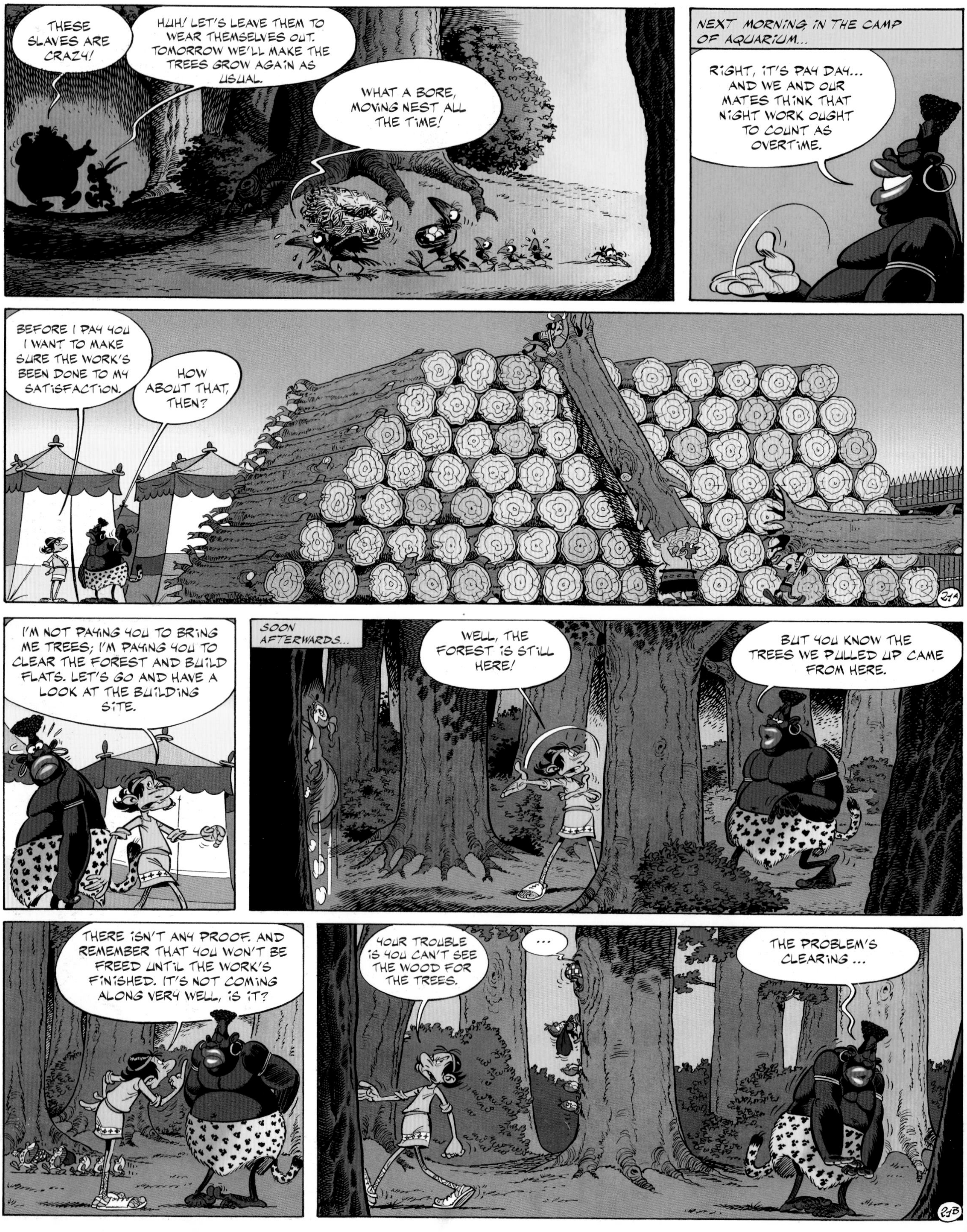
THESE SLAVES ARE CRAZY!
HUH! LET'S LEAVE THEM TO WEAR THEMSELVES OUT. TOMORROW WE'LL MAKE THE TREES GROW AGAIN AS USUAL.
WHAT A BORE, MOVING NEST ALL THE TIME!
NEXT MORNING IN THE CAMP OF AQUARIUM...
RIGHT, IT'S PAY DAY... AND WE AND OUR MATES THINK THAT NIGHT WORK OUGHT TO COUNT AS OVERTIME.
BEFORE I PAY YOU I WANT TO MAKE SURE THE WORK'S BEEN DONE TO MY SATISFACTION.
HOW ABOUT THAT, THEN?
I'M NOT PAYING YOU TO BRING ME TREES; I'M PAYING YOU TO CLEAR THE FOREST AND BUILD FLATS. LET'S GO AND HAVE A LOOK AT THE BUILDING SITE.
SOON AFTERWARDS...
WELL, THE FOREST IS STILL HERE!
BUT YOU KNOW THE TREES WE PULLED UP CAME FROM HERE.
THERE ISN'T ANY PROOF. AND REMEMBER THAT YOU WON'T BE FREED UNTIL THE WORK'S FINISHED. IT'S NOT COMING ALONG VERY WELL, IS IT?
YOUR TROUBLE IS YOU CAN'T SEE THE WOOD FOR THE TREES.
...
THE PROBLEM'S CLEARING ...

CENTURION! YOUR MEN ARE NOT DOING THEIR DUTY! THEY'LL HAVE TO GUARD THE SITE BY DAY TO STOP PEOPLE MAKING THE TREES GROW AGAIN AFTER WE PULL THEM UP BY NIGHT!

MY MEN ARE ON STRIKE, BUT NEGOTIATIONS HAVE NOT BROKEN DOWN. TODAY WE TACKLE THE QUESTION OF EVENING PASSES. THE DELEGATES WANT THEM EXTENDED BY AN HOUR.

MEANWHILE...

I WANT TO SEE YOUR CHIEF, GAUL.

HE'S IN HIS HUT, NUMIDIAN.

YOU'RE KEEPING US FROM BEING FREED BY NOT ALLOWING US TO FINISH THE WORK.

BUT WHEN YOU GO UPROOTING TREES YOU HURT DOGMATIX AND THE BOARS...

...AND THE BIRDS...

YES, WE CAN'T HAVE FOWL PLAY. IT'S THE ROMANS WE WANT TO GET THE BIRD.

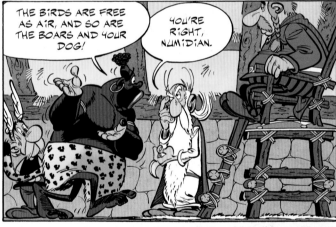

THE BIRDS ARE FREE AS AIR, AND SO ARE THE BOARS AND YOUR DOG!

YOU'RE RIGHT, NUMIDIAN.

NOT ONLY WILL WE STOP KEEPING YOU FROM FINISHING THE WORK, BUT I'LL GIVE YOU SOME MAGIC POTION TO HELP YOU GET IT DONE FASTER. COME ON!

DON'T WORRY; WE'RE GOING TO HAVE A BIT OF FUN WITH THE ROMANS. WE'LL TEACH THEM ANOTHER LESSON AND HELP THESE POOR SLAVES AT THE SAME TIME.

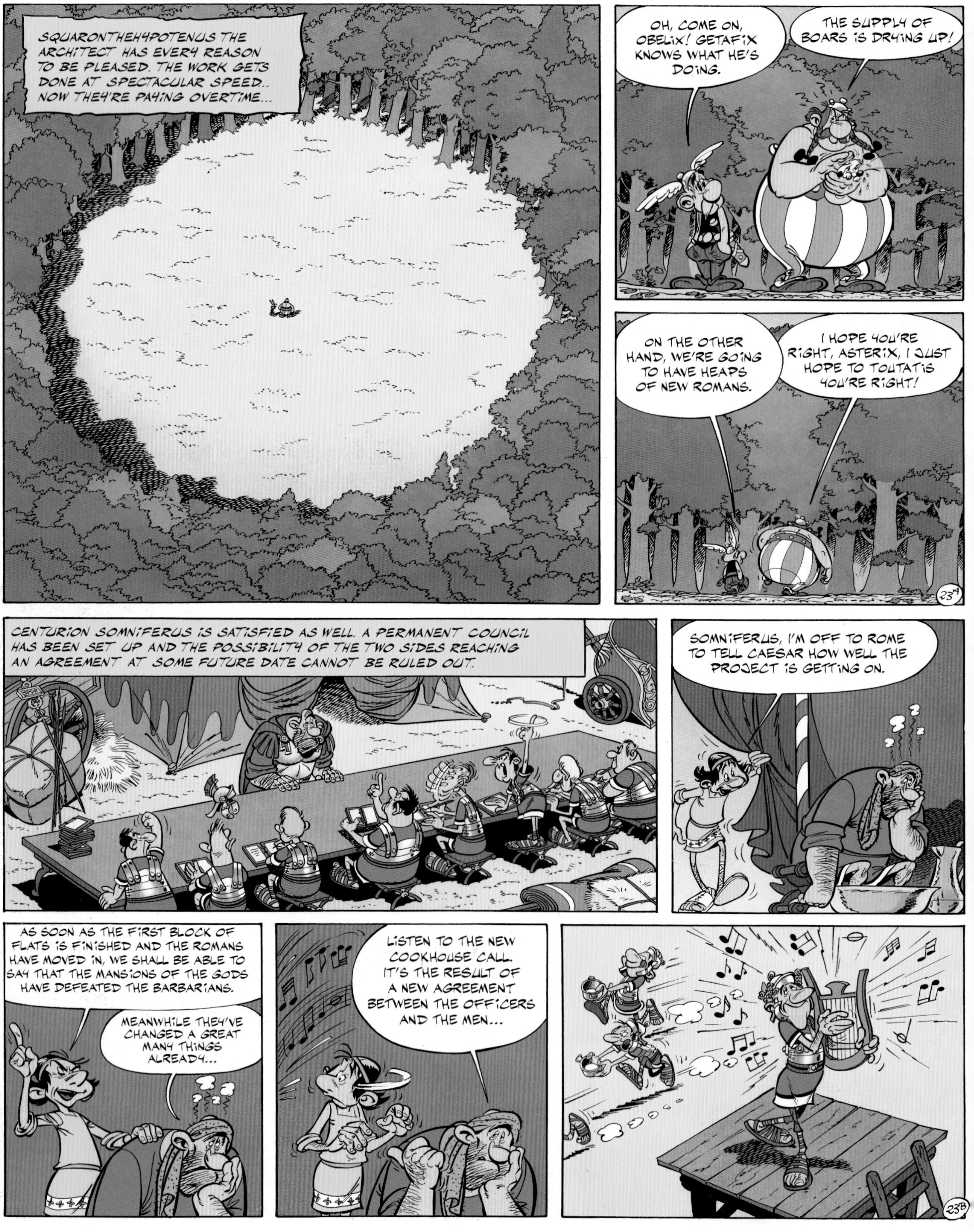
SQUARONTHEHYPOTENUS THE ARCHITECT HAS EVERY REASON TO BE PLEASED. THE WORK GETS DONE AT SPECTACULAR SPEED.. NOW THEY'RE PAYING OVERTIME...
OH, COME ON, OBELIX! GETAFIX KNOWS WHAT HE'S DOING.
THE SUPPLY OF BOARS IS DRYING UP!
ON THE OTHER HAND, WE'RE GOING TO HAVE HEAPS OF NEW ROMANS.
I HOPE YOU'RE RIGHT, ASTERIX, I JUST HOPE TO TOUTATIS YOU'RE RIGHT!
CENTURION SOMNIFERUS IS SATISFIED AS WELL. A PERMANENT COUNCIL HAS BEEN SET UP AND THE POSSIBILITY OF THE TWO SIDES REACHING AN AGREEMENT AT SOME FUTURE DATE CANNOT BE RULED OUT.
SOMNIFERUS, I'M OFF TO ROME TO TELL CAESAR HOW WELL THE PROJECT IS GETTING ON.
AS SOON AS THE FIRST BLOCK OF FLATS IS FINISHED AND THE ROMANS HAVE MOVED IN, WE SHALL BE ABLE TO SAY THAT THE MANSIONS OF THE GODS HAVE DEFEATED THE BARBARIANS.
MEANWHILE THEY'VE CHANGED A GREAT MANY THINGS ALREADY...
LISTEN TO THE NEW COOKHOUSE CALL. IT'S THE RESULT OF A NEW AGREEMENT BETWEEN THE OFFICERS AND THE MEN...

THE ARCHITECT SQUARONTHE-HYPOTENUS, BACK FROM GAUL, CRAVES AN AUDIENCE OF CAESAR!

SHOW HIM IN!

AVE, CAESAR! THE FIRST BUILDING IN THE MANSIONS OF THE GODS WILL SOON BE FINISHED!

IF WE SUCCEED IN GETTING ROMANS TO LIVE IN THE VICINITY OF THOSE GAULS, I CAN SAY NOT ONLY VENI AND VIDI, BUT REALLY VICI AS WELL!

I'VE PREPARED A PUBLICITY CAMPAIGN TO FIND TENANTS FOR THE MANSIONS OF THE GODS.

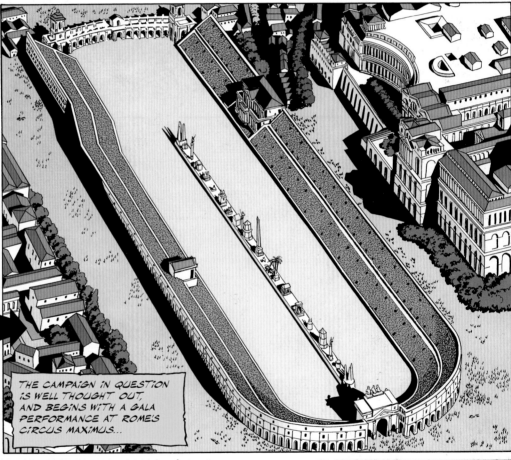

THE CAMPAIGN IN QUESTION IS WELL THOUGHT OUT, AND BEGINS WITH A GALA PERFORMANCE AT ROME'S CIRCUS MAXIMUS...

GALA PERFORMANCE

A GRAND RAFFLE
WILL BE HELD AT THE END
OF THE GLADIATORS' FIGHTS

THE WINNER WILL RECEIVE A FLAT IN
THE MANSIONS OF THE GODS

RETAIN THE NUMBERED TICKET
YOU RECEIVED AT THE TURNSTILE

THE MANSIONS OF THE GODS? WHAT IN THE NAME OF THE ELYSIAN FIELDS ARE THOSE?

PERHAPS WE'LL FIND OUT FROM THIS BROCHURE THEY HANDED US.

24

27

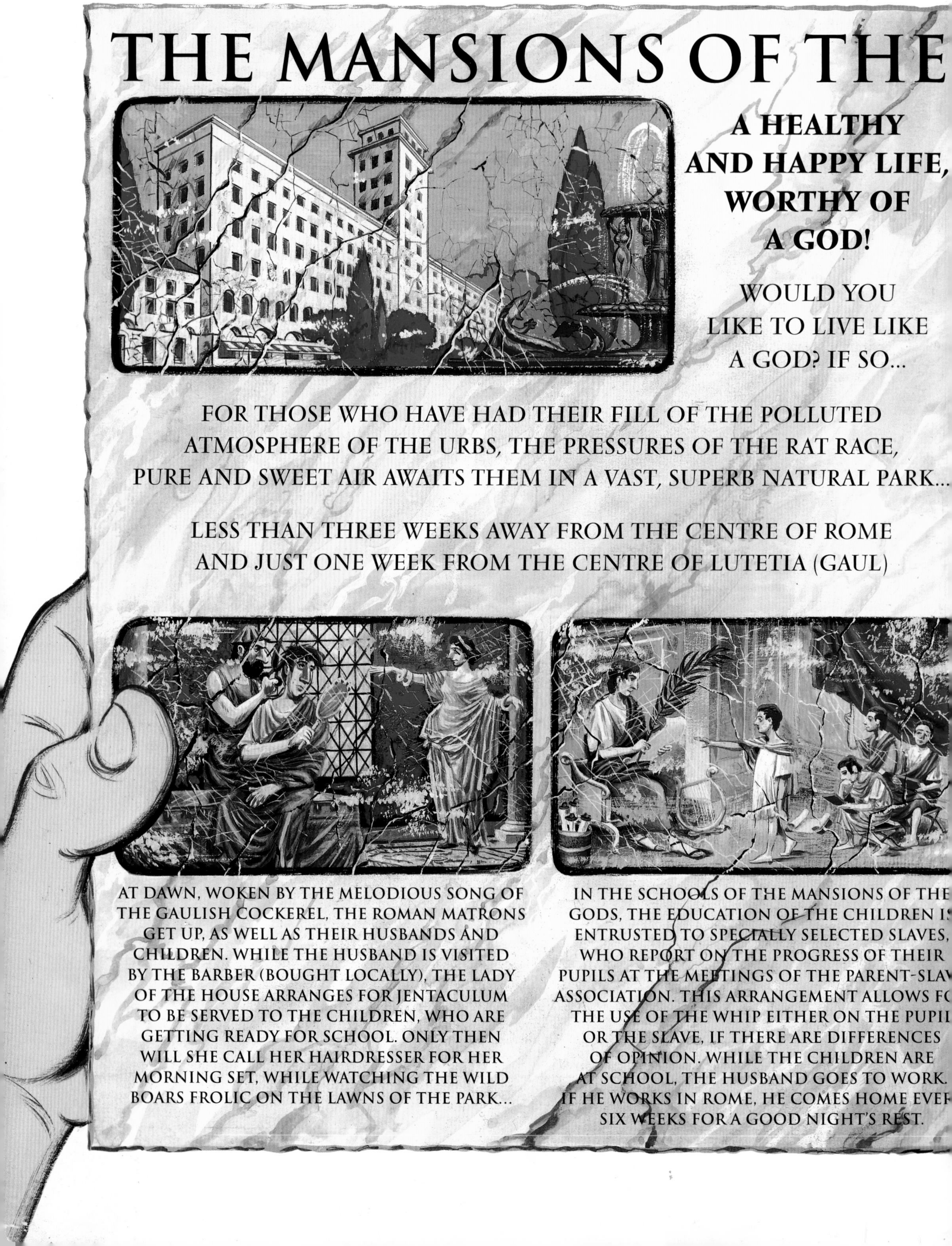
THE MANSIONS OF THE
A HEALTHY AND HAPPY LIFE, WORTHY OF A GOD!
WOULD YOU LIKE TO LIVE LIKE A GOD? IF SO...
FOR THOSE WHO HAVE HAD THEIR FILL OF THE POLLUTED ATMOSPHERE OF THE URBS, THE PRESSURES OF THE RAT RACE, PURE AND SWEET AIR AWAITS THEM IN A VAST, SUPERB NATURAL PARK...
LESS THAN THREE WEEKS AWAY FROM THE CENTRE OF ROME AND JUST ONE WEEK FROM THE CENTRE OF LUTETIA (GAUL)
AT DAWN, WOKEN BY THE MELODIOUS SONG OF THE GAULISH COCKEREL, THE ROMAN MATRONS GET UP, AS WELL AS THEIR HUSBANDS AND CHILDREN. WHILE THE HUSBAND IS VISITED BY THE BARBER (BOUGHT LOCALLY), THE LADY OF THE HOUSE ARRANGES FOR JENTACULUM TO BE SERVED TO THE CHILDREN, WHO ARE GETTING READY FOR SCHOOL. ONLY THEN WILL SHE CALL HER HAIRDRESSER FOR HER MORNING SET, WHILE WATCHING THE WILD BOARS FROLIC ON THE LAWNS OF THE PARK...
IN THE SCHOOLS OF THE MANSIONS OF THE GODS, THE EDUCATION OF THE CHILDREN I ENTRUSTED TO SPECIALLY SELECTED SLAVES, WHO REPORT ON THE PROGRESS OF THEIR PUPILS AT THE MEETINGS OF THE PARENT-SLAV ASSOCIATION. THIS ARRANGEMENT ALLOWS FO THE USE OF THE WHIP EITHER ON THE PUPI OR THE SLAVE, IF THERE ARE DIFFERENCES OF OPINION. WHILE THE CHILDREN ARE AT SCHOOL, THE HUSBAND GOES TO WORK. IF HE WORKS IN ROME, HE COMES HOME EVER SIX WEEKS FOR A GOOD NIGHT'S REST.

GODS ARE FOR YOU!

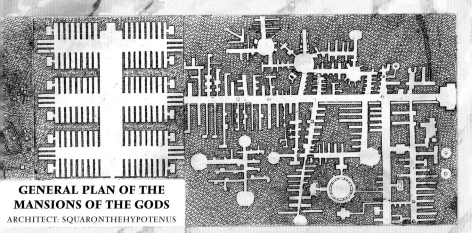

GENERAL PLAN OF THE MANSIONS OF THE GODS
ARCHITECT: SQUARONTHEHYPOTENUS

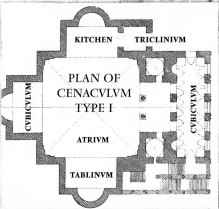

KITCHEN · TRICLINIVM

PLAN OF CENACVLVM TYPE I

CVBICVLVM · CVBICVLVM

ATRIVM

TABLINVM

SHOPPING PRECINCT TO BE CONSTRUCTED

BATHS AND SPORTS HALL TO BE CONSTRUCTED

GAVLISEVM TO BE CONSTRUCTED

ONCE HER HUSBAND AND CHILDREN HAVE GONE, THE MATRON VISITS HER FRIENDS FOR XISES. AFTERWARDS SHE MAY GO TO THE SHOPPING PRECINCT (TO BE CONSTRUCTED) WHERE SHE CAN FIND ALL SHE NEEDS, FROM FOOD AND CLOTHES TO JEWELLERY AND SLAVES. SHE IS HAVING A DINNER PARTY, AND SHE'S ONE SLAVE SHORT? SHE GOES STRAIGHT TO THE SELF-SERVICE SLAVE MARKET! SOON THE FAMILY WILL BE HOME. IT IS TIME TO PREPARE THE CENA.

WHEN THE HUSBAND COMES HOME FROM WORK HE CAN VISIT THE BATHS AND THE SPORTS HALL WITH HIS FRIENDS, OR GO FOR A ROMANTIC STROLL WITH HIS WIFE ALONG THE SHADY FOOTPATHS OF THE PARK (WHERE THE WILD BOARS FROLIC). IN THE EVENING, HE CAN GO TO THE GAULISEUM (TO BE CONSTRUCTED), OR SIMPLY HAVE A FEW FRIENDS IN FOR AN ORGY. ALL HE HAS TO DO THEN IS GO TO BED AND AWAIT THE DAWNING OF A MAGNIFICENT NEW DAY, THE SORT OF DAY YOU CAN FIND ONLY IN THE MANSIONS OF THE GODS!

26

THAT'S ALL VERY WELL, BUT I SEEM TO REMEMBER THAT THERE ARE PARTS OF GAUL WHICH ARE NOT VERY RESTFUL...

OH, IT'S IN GAUL, IS IT?

THE LAST PAIR OF GLADIATORS HAVE FINISHED MASSACRING EACH OTHER, AND SHOWBUSINUS, THE FAMOUS MASTER OF CEREMONIES, COMES TO THE CENTRE OF THE ARENA.

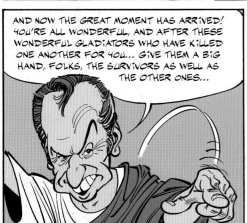

AND NOW THE GREAT MOMENT HAS ARRIVED! YOU'RE ALL WONDERFUL, AND AFTER THESE WONDERFUL GLADIATORS WHO HAVE KILLED ONE ANOTHER FOR YOU... GIVE THEM A BIG HAND, FOLKS, THE SURVIVORS AS WELL AS THE OTHER ONES...

THANK YOU... WE'RE GOING TO PICK THE FORTUNATE WINNER OF ONE OF THE CENACULA IN THE MANSIONS OF THE GODS... WE HAVE HERE A WONDERFUL VESTAL VIRGIN – GIVE HER A BIG HAND, FOLKS! SHE WILL DRAW THE WINNING NUMBER.

CLAP CLAPCLAPCLAPCLAP CLAPCLAP

CIV! WHO HAS GOT CIV?

IT'S YOU!

SHHHHHH!

HERE HE IS! OVER HERE!

AH, I SEE WE HAVE A WONDERFUL WINNER! COME DOWN INTO THE ARENA, PLEASE!

GIVE HIM A BIG HAND, FOLKS!

WHAT IF I REFUSE TO GO TO GAUL?

YOU'LL STAY IN THE ARENA AND WE'LL LET IN THE LIONS.

IN THAT CASE, I ACCEPT.

DID YOU HEAR THAT?

HE ACCEPTS! GIVE THIS WONDERFUL WINNER A BIG HAND, FOLKS!!!

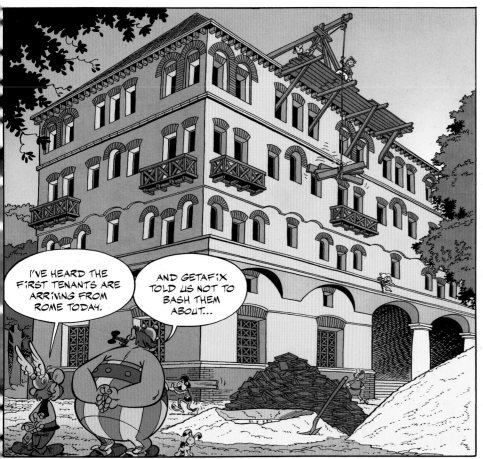

I'VE HEARD THE FIRST TENANTS ARE ARRIVING FROM ROME TODAY.

AND GETAFIX TOLD US NOT TO BASH THEM ABOUT...

I'M VERY WORRIED ABOUT THESE ROMANS, GETAFIX.

THEY MAY BE WONDERFUL...

I KNOW WHAT LINE I'M TAKING: I SHALL IGNORE THEM!

SO SHALL I!

I CAN'T THINK WHAT'S STOPPING ME KNOCKING THEIR BLASTED FLATS DOWN!

TAKE IT EASY! AT LEAST THE SLAVES HAVE BEEN FREED. THAT'S ONE GOOD THING!

SURE ENOUGH...

WHAT ARE WE GOING TO DO NOW WE'RE FREE?

NOW OUR SHIP'S COME HOME, WE'LL FLOAT A COMPANY, ME HEARTIES!

CLING! CLING!

WELCOME TO THE MANSIONS OF THE GODS!

31

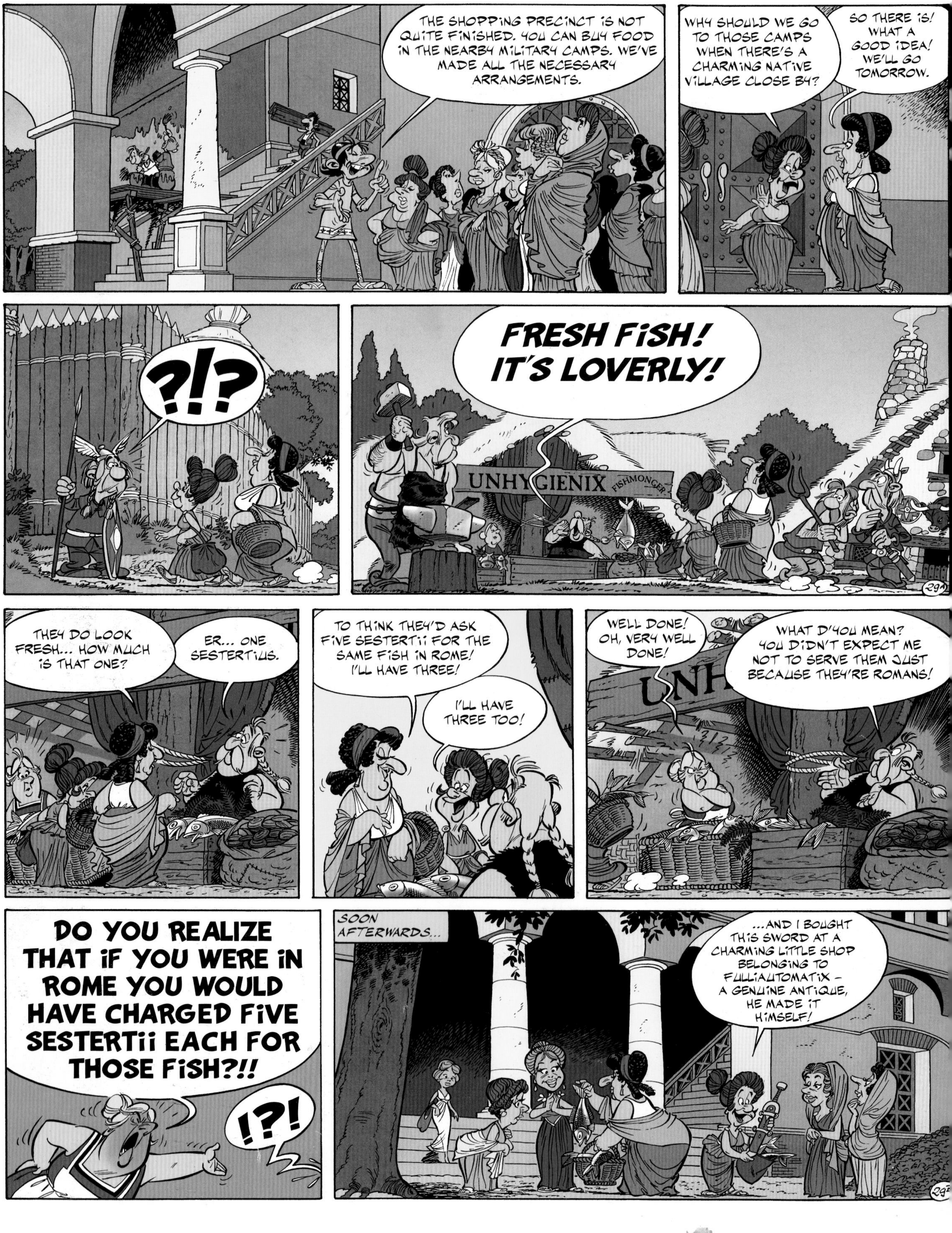
THE SHOPPING PRECINCT IS NOT QUITE FINISHED. YOU CAN BUY FOOD IN THE NEARBY MILITARY CAMPS. WE'VE MADE ALL THE NECESSARY ARRANGEMENTS.
WHY SHOULD WE GO TO THOSE CAMPS WHEN THERE'S A CHARMING NATIVE VILLAGE CLOSE BY?
SO THERE IS! WHAT A GOOD IDEA! WE'LL GO TOMORROW.
?!?
FRESH FISH! IT'S LOVERLY!
UNHYGIENIX
FISHMONGER
THEY DO LOOK FRESH... HOW MUCH IS THAT ONE?
ER... ONE SESTERTIUS.
TO THINK THEY'D ASK FIVE SESTERTII FOR THE SAME FISH IN ROME! I'LL HAVE THREE!
I'LL HAVE THREE TOO!
WELL DONE! OH, VERY WELL DONE!
WHAT D'YOU MEAN? YOU DIDN'T EXPECT ME NOT TO SERVE THEM JUST BECAUSE THEY'RE ROMANS!
DO YOU REALIZE THAT IF YOU WERE IN ROME YOU WOULD HAVE CHARGED FIVE SESTERTII EACH FOR THOSE FISH?!!
!?!
SOON AFTERWARDS...
...AND I BOUGHT THIS SWORD AT A CHARMING LITTLE SHOP BELONGING TO FULLIAUTOMATIX – A GENUINE ANTIQUE, HE MADE IT HIMSELF!

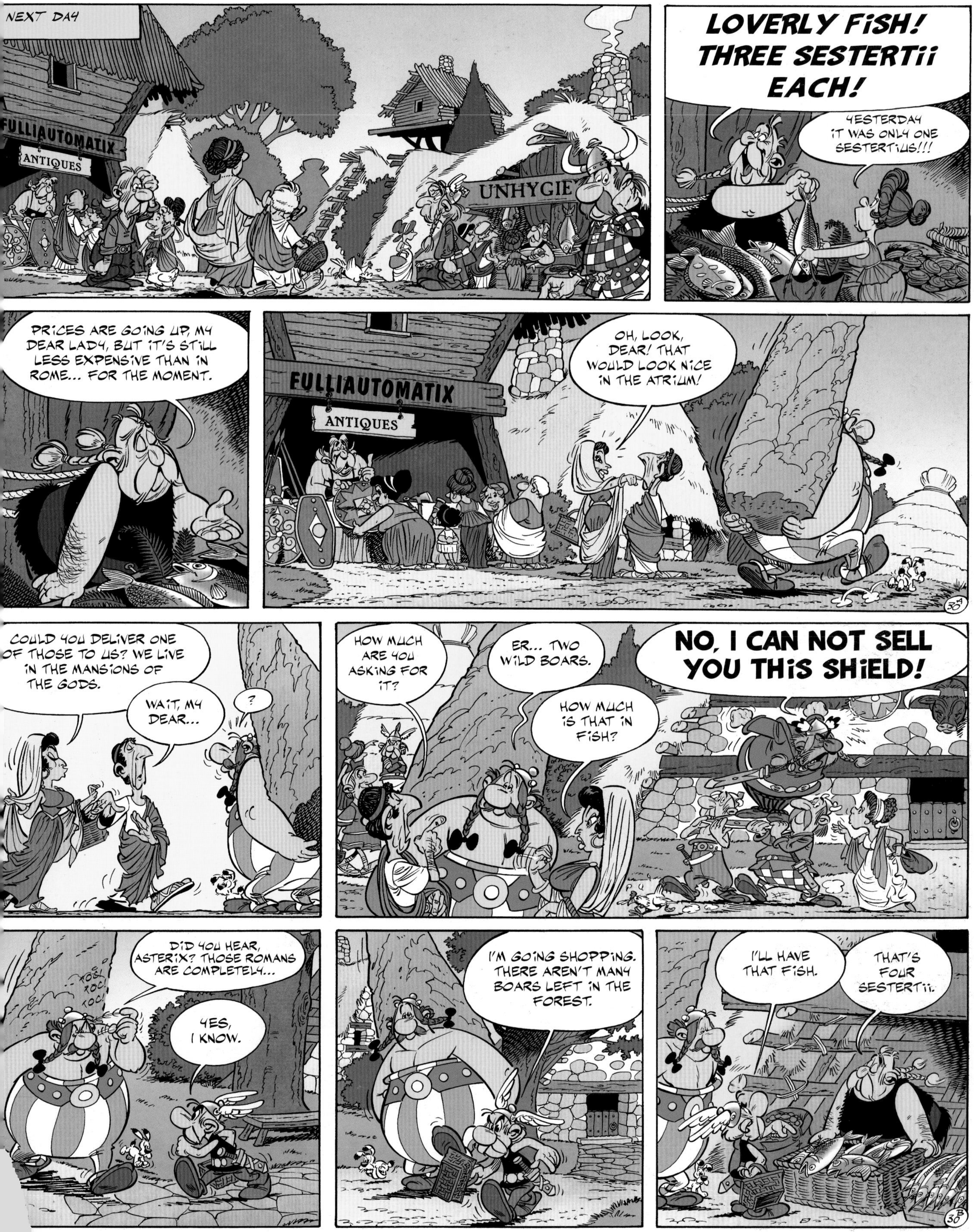
NEXT DAY
FULLIAUTOMATIX
ANTIQUES
UNHYGIE
LOVERLY FiSH! THREE SESTERTii EACH!
YESTERDAY iT WAS ONLY ONE SESTERTiUS!!!
PRiCES ARE GOiNG UP, MY DEAR LADY, BUT iT'S STiLL LESS EXPENSiVE THAN iN ROME... FOR THE MOMENT.
FULLIAUTOMATIX
ANTIQUES
OH, LOOK, DEAR! THAT WOULD LOOK NiCE iN THE ATRiUM!
COULD YOU DELiVER ONE OF THOSE TO US? WE LiVE iN THE MANSiONS OF THE GODS.
WAiT, MY DEAR...
?
HOW MUCH ARE YOU ASKiNG FOR iT?
ER... TWO WiLD BOARS.
HOW MUCH iS THAT iN FiSH?
NO, I CAN NOT SELL YOU THiS SHiELD!
DiD YOU HEAR, ASTERiX? THOSE ROMANS ARE COMPLETELY...
YES, I KNOW.
I'M GOiNG SHOPPiNG. THERE AREN'T MANY BOARS LEFT iN THE FOREST.
I'LL HAVE THAT FiSH.
THAT'S FOUR SESTERTii.

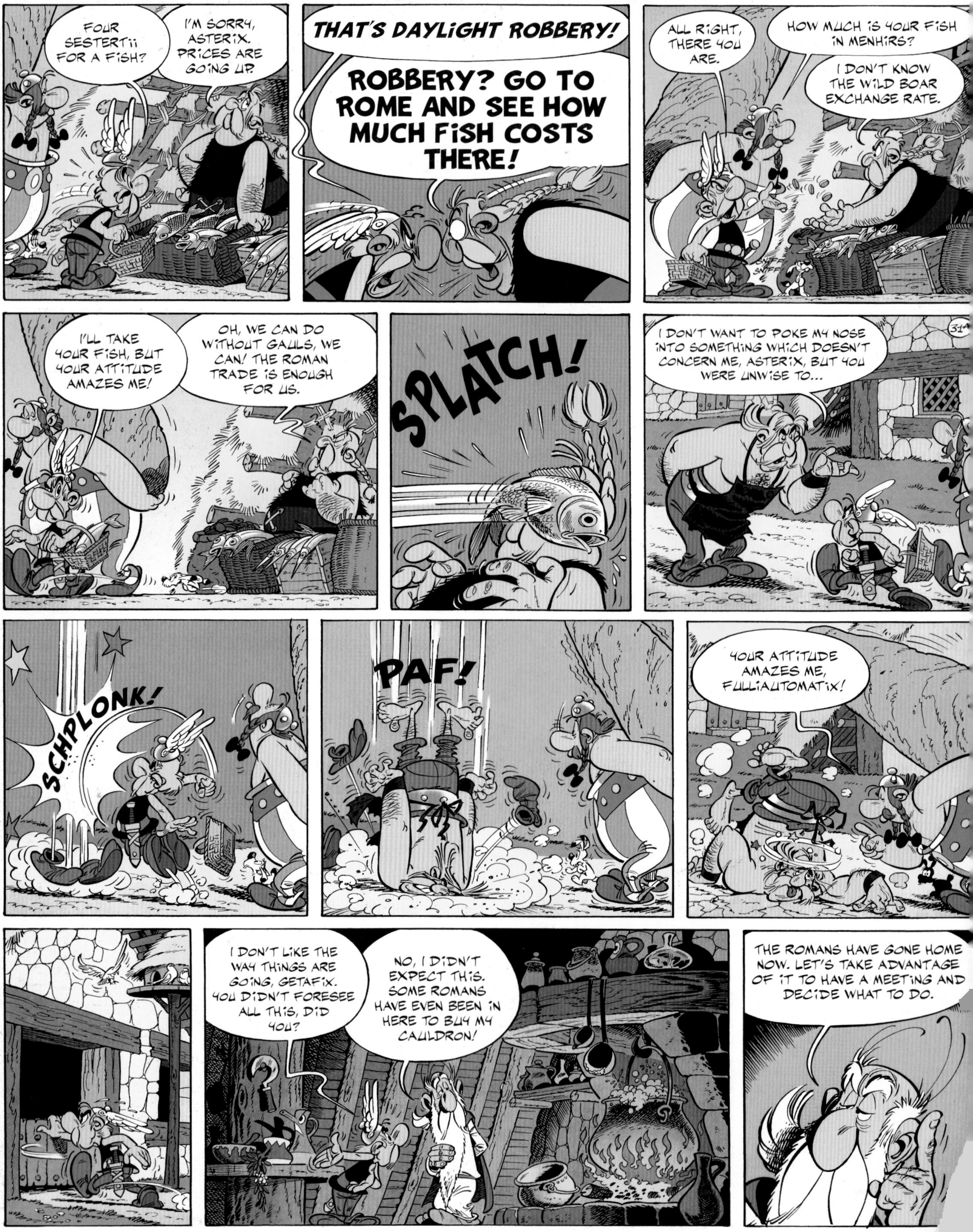

FOUR SESTERTII FOR A FISH?
I'M SORRY, ASTERIX. PRICES ARE GOING UP.
THAT'S DAYLIGHT ROBBERY!
ROBBERY? GO TO ROME AND SEE HOW MUCH FISH COSTS THERE!
ALL RIGHT, THERE YOU ARE.
HOW MUCH IS YOUR FISH IN MENHIRS?
I DON'T KNOW THE WILD BOAR EXCHANGE RATE.
SNIFF SNIFF
I'LL TAKE YOUR FISH, BUT YOUR ATTITUDE AMAZES ME!
OH, WE CAN DO WITHOUT GAULS, WE CAN! THE ROMAN TRADE IS ENOUGH FOR US.
SPLATCH!
I DON'T WANT TO POKE MY NOSE INTO SOMETHING WHICH DOESN'T CONCERN ME, ASTERIX, BUT YOU WERE UNWISE TO...
SCHPLONK!
PAF!
YOUR ATTITUDE AMAZES ME, FULLIAUTOMATIX!
I DON'T LIKE THE WAY THINGS ARE GOING, GETAFIX. YOU DIDN'T FORESEE ALL THIS, DID YOU?
NO, I DIDN'T EXPECT THIS. SOME ROMANS HAVE EVEN BEEN IN HERE TO BUY MY CAULDRON!
THE ROMANS HAVE GONE HOME NOW. LET'S TAKE ADVANTAGE OF IT TO HAVE A MEETING AND DECIDE WHAT TO DO.

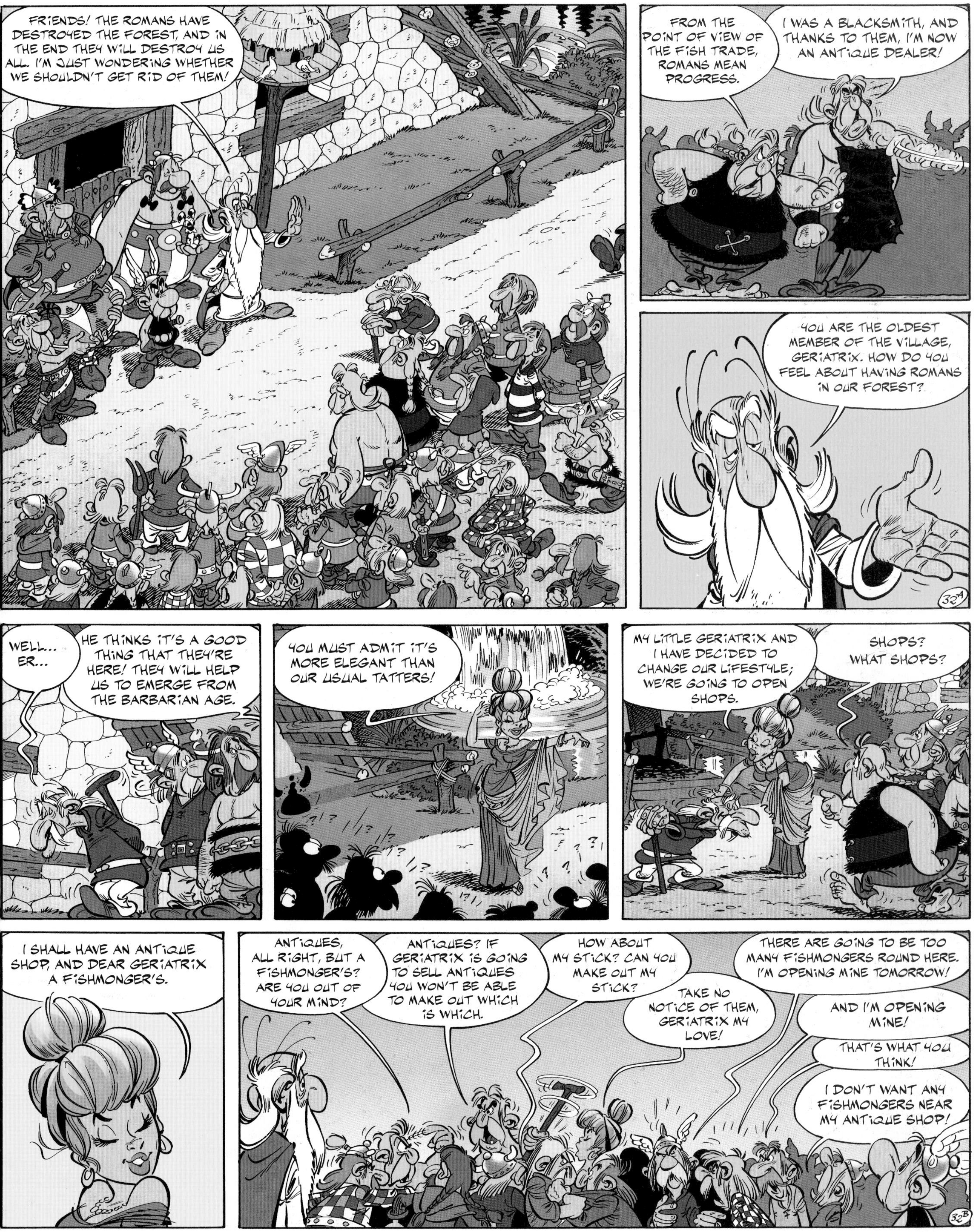
FRIENDS! THE ROMANS HAVE DESTROYED THE FOREST, AND IN THE END THEY WILL DESTROY US ALL. I'M JUST WONDERING WHETHER WE SHOULDN'T GET RID OF THEM!
FROM THE POINT OF VIEW OF THE FISH TRADE, ROMANS MEAN PROGRESS.
I WAS A BLACKSMITH, AND THANKS TO THEM, I'M NOW AN ANTIQUE DEALER!
YOU ARE THE OLDEST MEMBER OF THE VILLAGE, GERIATRIX. HOW DO YOU FEEL ABOUT HAVING ROMANS IN OUR FOREST?
WELL... ER...
HE THINKS IT'S A GOOD THING THAT THEY'RE HERE! THEY WILL HELP US TO EMERGE FROM THE BARBARIAN AGE.
YOU MUST ADMIT IT'S MORE ELEGANT THAN OUR USUAL TATTERS!
MY LITTLE GERIATRIX AND I HAVE DECIDED TO CHANGE OUR LIFESTYLE; WE'RE GOING TO OPEN SHOPS.
SHOPS? WHAT SHOPS?
I SHALL HAVE AN ANTIQUE SHOP, AND DEAR GERIATRIX A FISHMONGER'S.
ANTIQUES, ALL RIGHT, BUT A FISHMONGER'S? ARE YOU OUT OF YOUR MIND?
ANTIQUES? IF GERIATRIX IS GOING TO SELL ANTIQUES YOU WON'T BE ABLE TO MAKE OUT WHICH IS WHICH.
HOW ABOUT MY STICK? CAN YOU MAKE OUT MY STICK?
TAKE NO NOTICE OF THEM, GERIATRIX MY LOVE!
THERE ARE GOING TO BE TOO MANY FISHMONGERS ROUND HERE. I'M OPENING MINE TOMORROW!
AND I'M OPENING MINE!
THAT'S WHAT YOU THINK!
I DON'T WANT ANY FISHMONGERS NEAR MY ANTIQUE SHOP!

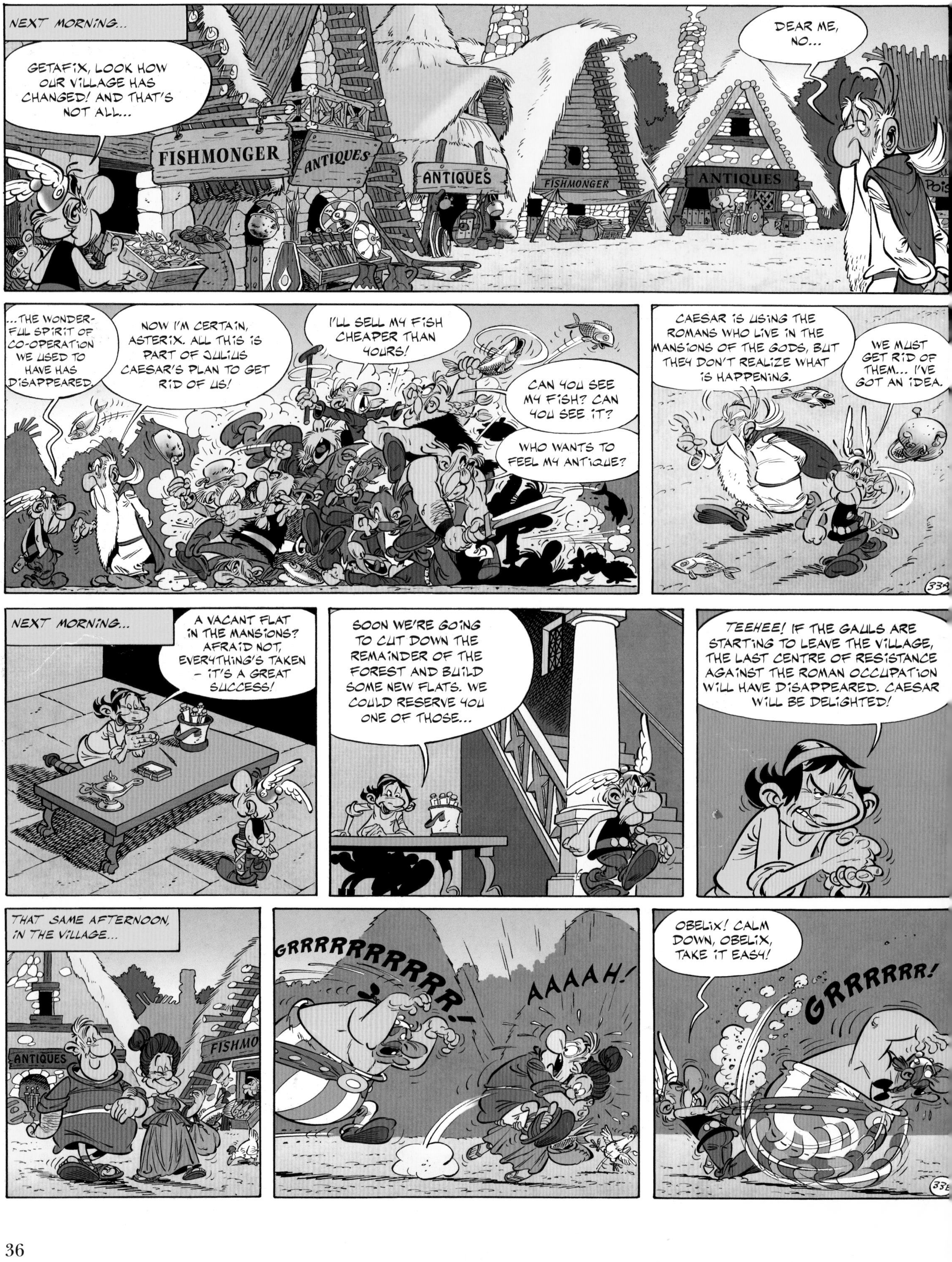
NEXT MORNING...
GETAFIX, LOOK HOW OUR VILLAGE HAS CHANGED! AND THAT'S NOT ALL...
DEAR ME, NO...
FISHMONGER
ANTIQUES
ANTIQUES
FISHMONGER
ANTIQUES
...THE WONDERFUL SPIRIT OF CO-OPERATION WE USED TO HAVE HAS DISAPPEARED.
NOW I'M CERTAIN, ASTERIX. ALL THIS IS PART OF JULIUS CAESAR'S PLAN TO GET RID OF US!
I'LL SELL MY FISH CHEAPER THAN YOURS!
CAN YOU SEE MY FISH? CAN YOU SEE IT?
WHO WANTS TO FEEL MY ANTIQUE?
CAESAR IS USING THE ROMANS WHO LIVE IN THE MANSIONS OF THE GODS, BUT THEY DON'T REALIZE WHAT IS HAPPENING.
WE MUST GET RID OF THEM... I'VE GOT AN IDEA.
NEXT MORNING...
A VACANT FLAT IN THE MANSIONS? AFRAID NOT, EVERYTHING'S TAKEN - IT'S A GREAT SUCCESS!
SOON WE'RE GOING TO CUT DOWN THE REMAINDER OF THE FOREST AND BUILD SOME NEW FLATS. WE COULD RESERVE YOU ONE OF THOSE...
TEEHEE! IF THE GAULS ARE STARTING TO LEAVE THE VILLAGE, THE LAST CENTRE OF RESISTANCE AGAINST THE ROMAN OCCUPATION WILL HAVE DISAPPEARED. CAESAR WILL BE DELIGHTED!
THAT SAME AFTERNOON, IN THE VILLAGE...
ANTIQUES
FISHMO
GRRRRRRRRRRRR!
AAAAH!
OBELIX! CALM DOWN, OBELIX, TAKE IT EASY!
GRRRRRR!

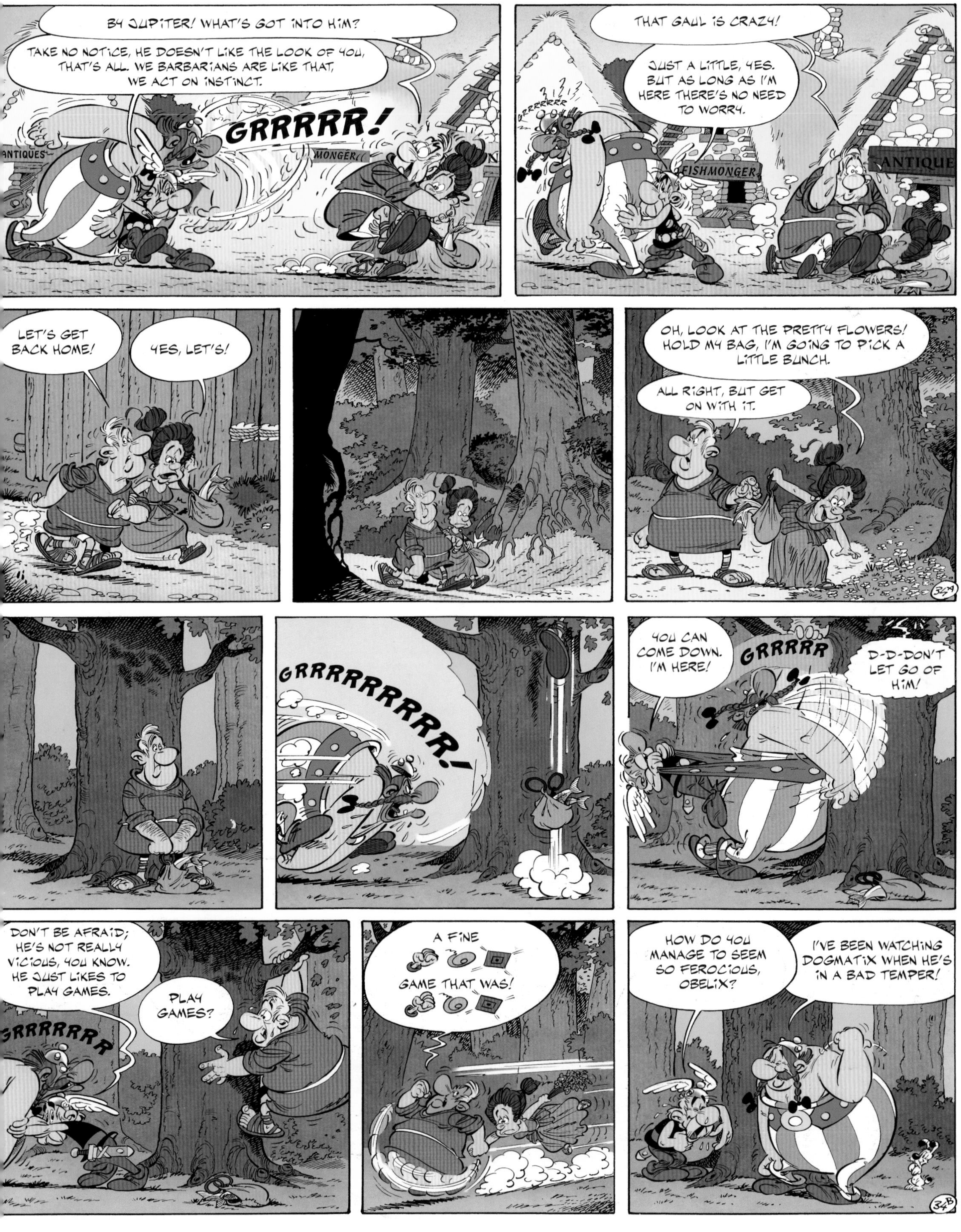

BY JUPITER! WHAT'S GOT INTO HIM?
TAKE NO NOTICE, HE DOESN'T LIKE THE LOOK OF YOU, THAT'S ALL. WE BARBARIANS ARE LIKE THAT, WE ACT ON INSTINCT.
GRRRRR!
ANTIQUES
MONGER
THAT GAUL IS CRAZY!
JUST A LITTLE, YES. BUT AS LONG AS I'M HERE THERE'S NO NEED TO WORRY.
GRRRRRRR
FISHMONGER
ANTIQUE
LET'S GET BACK HOME!
YES, LET'S!
OH, LOOK AT THE PRETTY FLOWERS! HOLD MY BAG, I'M GOING TO PICK A LITTLE BUNCH.
ALL RIGHT, BUT GET ON WITH IT.
GRRRRRRRRRRR!
YOU CAN COME DOWN. I'M HERE!
GRRRRR
D-D-DON'T LET GO OF HIM!
DON'T BE AFRAID; HE'S NOT REALLY VICIOUS, YOU KNOW. HE JUST LIKES TO PLAY GAMES.
GRRRRRRR
PLAY GAMES?
A FINE GAME THAT WAS!
HOW DO YOU MANAGE TO SEEM SO FEROCIOUS, OBELIX?
I'VE BEEN WATCHING DOGMATIX WHEN HE'S IN A BAD TEMPER!

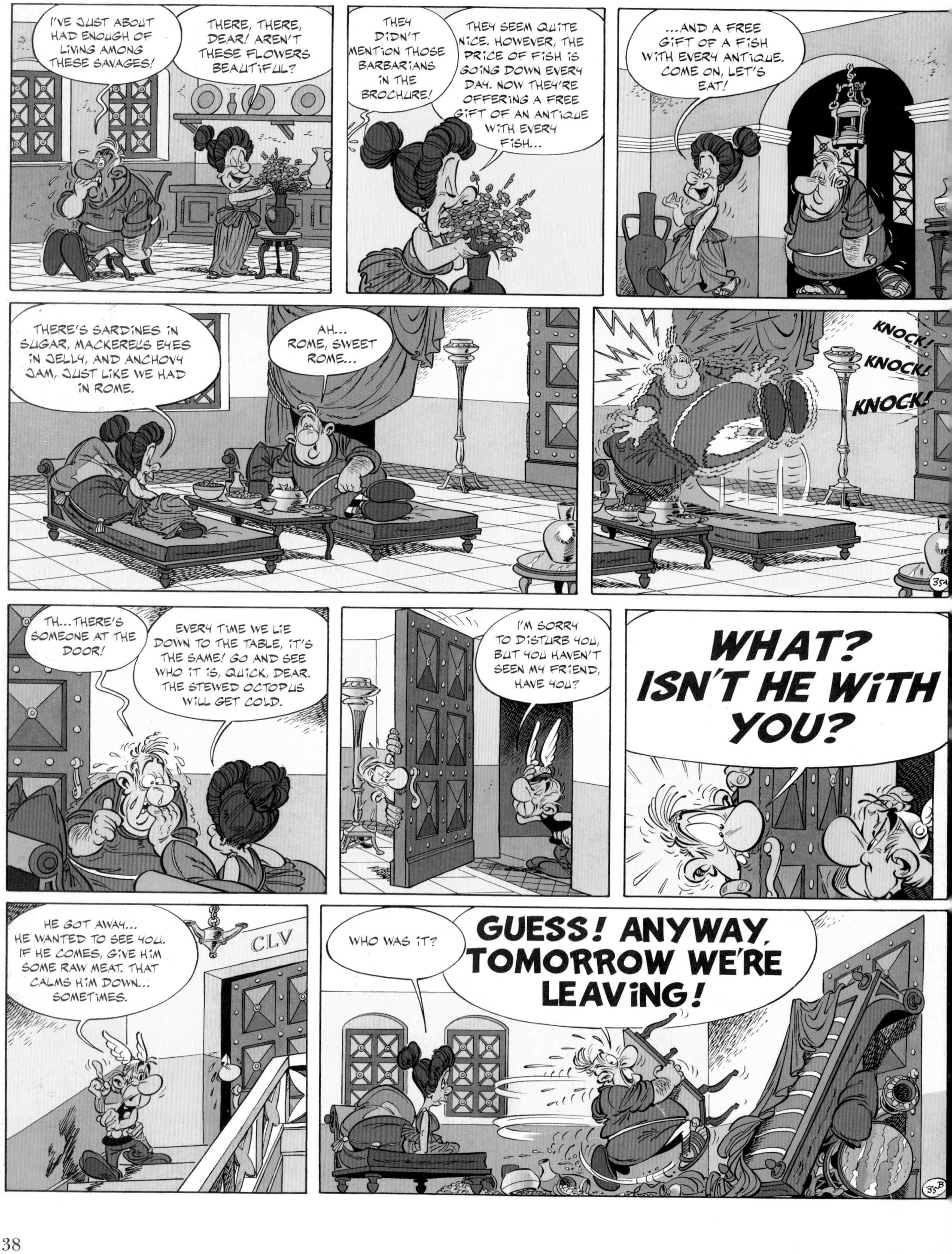
I'VE JUST ABOUT HAD ENOUGH OF LIVING AMONG THESE SAVAGES!
THERE, THERE, DEAR! AREN'T THESE FLOWERS BEAUTIFUL?
THEY DIDN'T MENTION THOSE BARBARIANS IN THE BROCHURE!
THEY SEEM QUITE NICE. HOWEVER, THE PRICE OF FISH IS GOING DOWN EVERY DAY. NOW THEY'RE OFFERING A FREE GIFT OF AN ANTIQUE WITH EVERY FISH...
...AND A FREE GIFT OF A FISH WITH EVERY ANTIQUE. COME ON, LET'S EAT!
THERE'S SARDINES IN SUGAR, MACKEREL'S EYES IN JELLY, AND ANCHOVY JAM, JUST LIKE WE HAD IN ROME.
AH... ROME, SWEET ROME...
KNOCK! KNOCK! KNOCK!
TH... THERE'S SOMEONE AT THE DOOR!
EVERY TIME WE LIE DOWN TO THE TABLE, IT'S THE SAME! GO AND SEE WHO IT IS, QUICK, DEAR. THE STEWED OCTOPUS WILL GET COLD.
I'M SORRY TO DISTURB YOU, BUT YOU HAVEN'T SEEN MY FRIEND, HAVE YOU?
WHAT? ISN'T HE WITH YOU?
HE GOT AWAY... HE WANTED TO SEE YOU. IF HE COMES, GIVE HIM SOME RAW MEAT. THAT CALMS HIM DOWN... SOMETIMES.
CLV
WHO WAS IT?
GUESS! ANYWAY, TOMORROW WE'RE LEAVING!

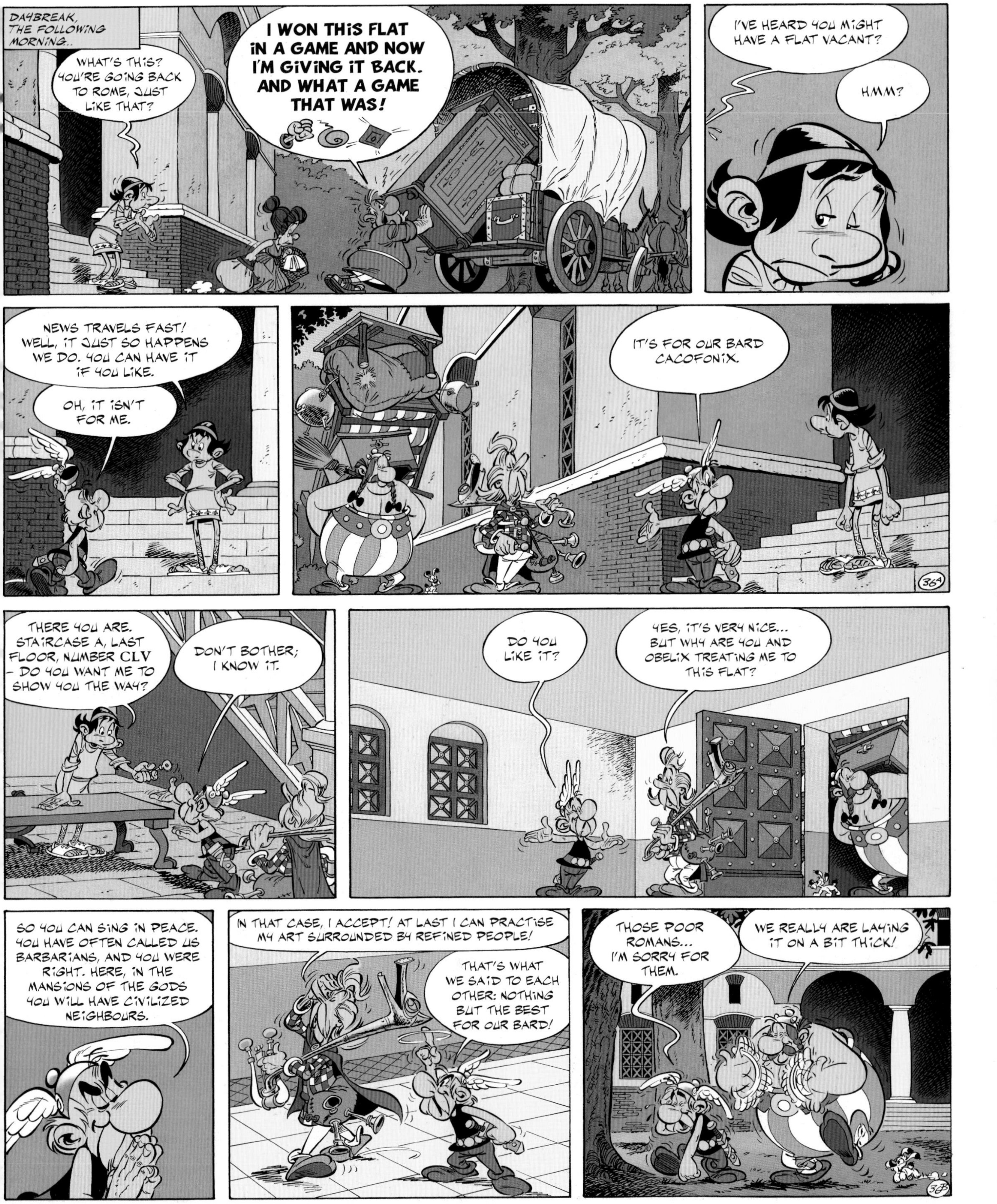
DAYBREAK, THE FOLLOWING MORNING...
WHAT'S THIS? YOU'RE GOING BACK TO ROME, JUST LIKE THAT?
I WON THIS FLAT IN A GAME AND NOW I'M GIVING IT BACK. AND WHAT A GAME THAT WAS!
I'VE HEARD YOU MIGHT HAVE A FLAT VACANT?
HMM?
NEWS TRAVELS FAST! WELL, IT JUST SO HAPPENS WE DO. YOU CAN HAVE IT IF YOU LIKE.
OH, IT ISN'T FOR ME.
IT'S FOR OUR BARD CACOFONIX.
THERE YOU ARE. STAIRCASE A, LAST FLOOR, NUMBER CLV - DO YOU WANT ME TO SHOW YOU THE WAY?
DON'T BOTHER; I KNOW IT.
DO YOU LIKE IT?
YES, IT'S VERY NICE... BUT WHY ARE YOU AND OBELIX TREATING ME TO THIS FLAT?
SO YOU CAN SING IN PEACE. YOU HAVE OFTEN CALLED US BARBARIANS, AND YOU WERE RIGHT. HERE, IN THE MANSIONS OF THE GODS YOU WILL HAVE CIVILIZED NEIGHBOURS.
IN THAT CASE, I ACCEPT! AT LAST I CAN PRACTISE MY ART SURROUNDED BY REFINED PEOPLE!
THAT'S WHAT WE SAID TO EACH OTHER: NOTHING BUT THE BEST FOR OUR BARD!
THOSE POOR ROMANS... I'M SORRY FOR THEM.
WE REALLY ARE LAYING IT ON A BIT THICK!

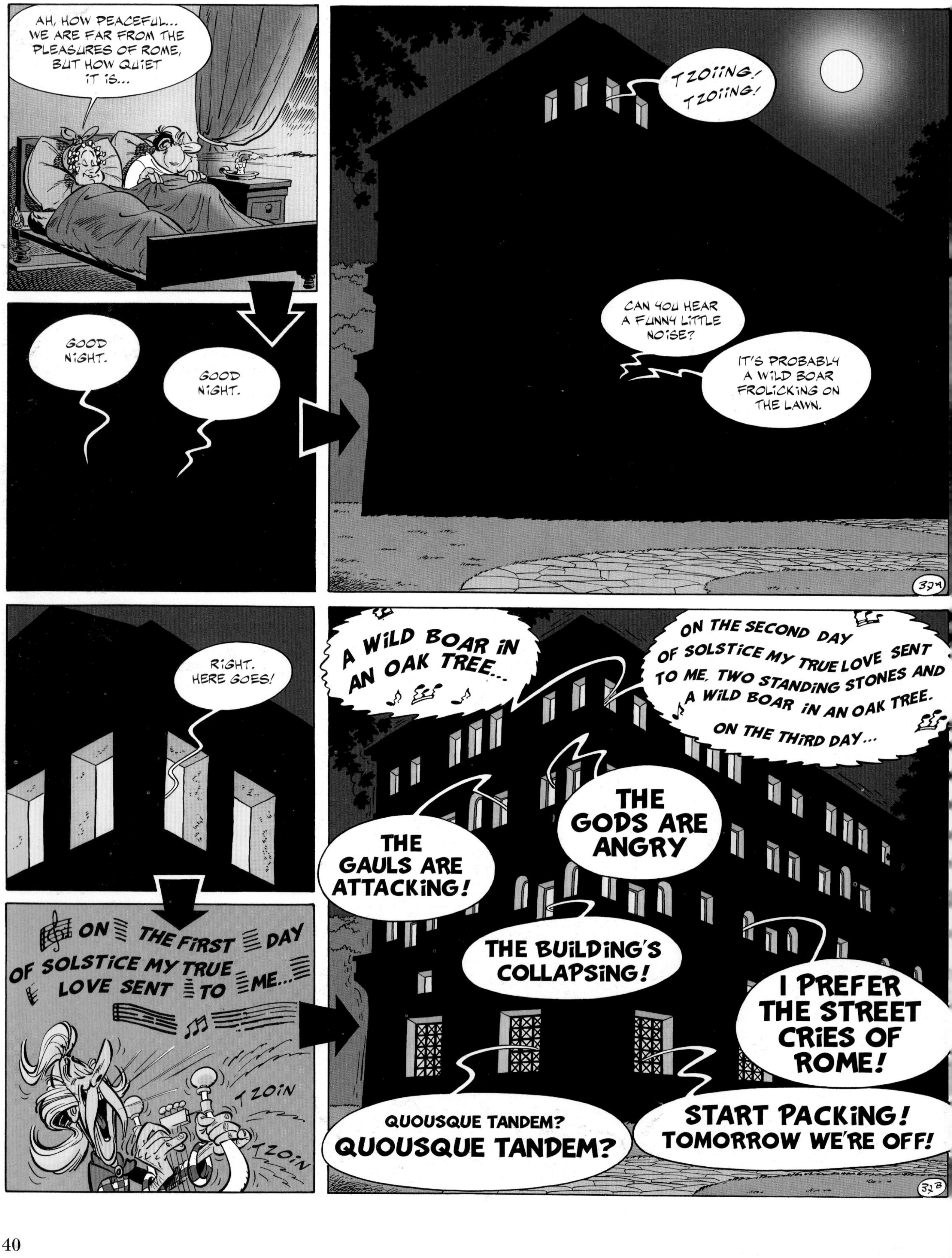

AH, HOW PEACEFUL... WE ARE FAR FROM THE PLEASURES OF ROME, BUT HOW QUIET IT IS...
TZOIING! TZOIING!
GOOD NIGHT.
GOOD NIGHT.
CAN YOU HEAR A FUNNY LITTLE NOISE?
IT'S PROBABLY A WILD BOAR FROLICKING ON THE LAWN.
RIGHT. HERE GOES!
ON THE FIRST DAY OF SOLSTICE MY TRUE LOVE SENT TO ME...
TZOIN
TZOIN
A WILD BOAR IN AN OAK TREE...
ON THE SECOND DAY OF SOLSTICE MY TRUE LOVE SENT TO ME, TWO STANDING STONES AND A WILD BOAR IN AN OAK TREE.
ON THE THIRD DAY...
THE GAULS ARE ATTACKING!
THE GODS ARE ANGRY
THE BUILDING'S COLLAPSING!
I PREFER THE STREET CRIES OF ROME!
QUOUSQUE TANDEM? QUOUSQUE TANDEM?
START PACKING! TOMORROW WE'RE OFF!

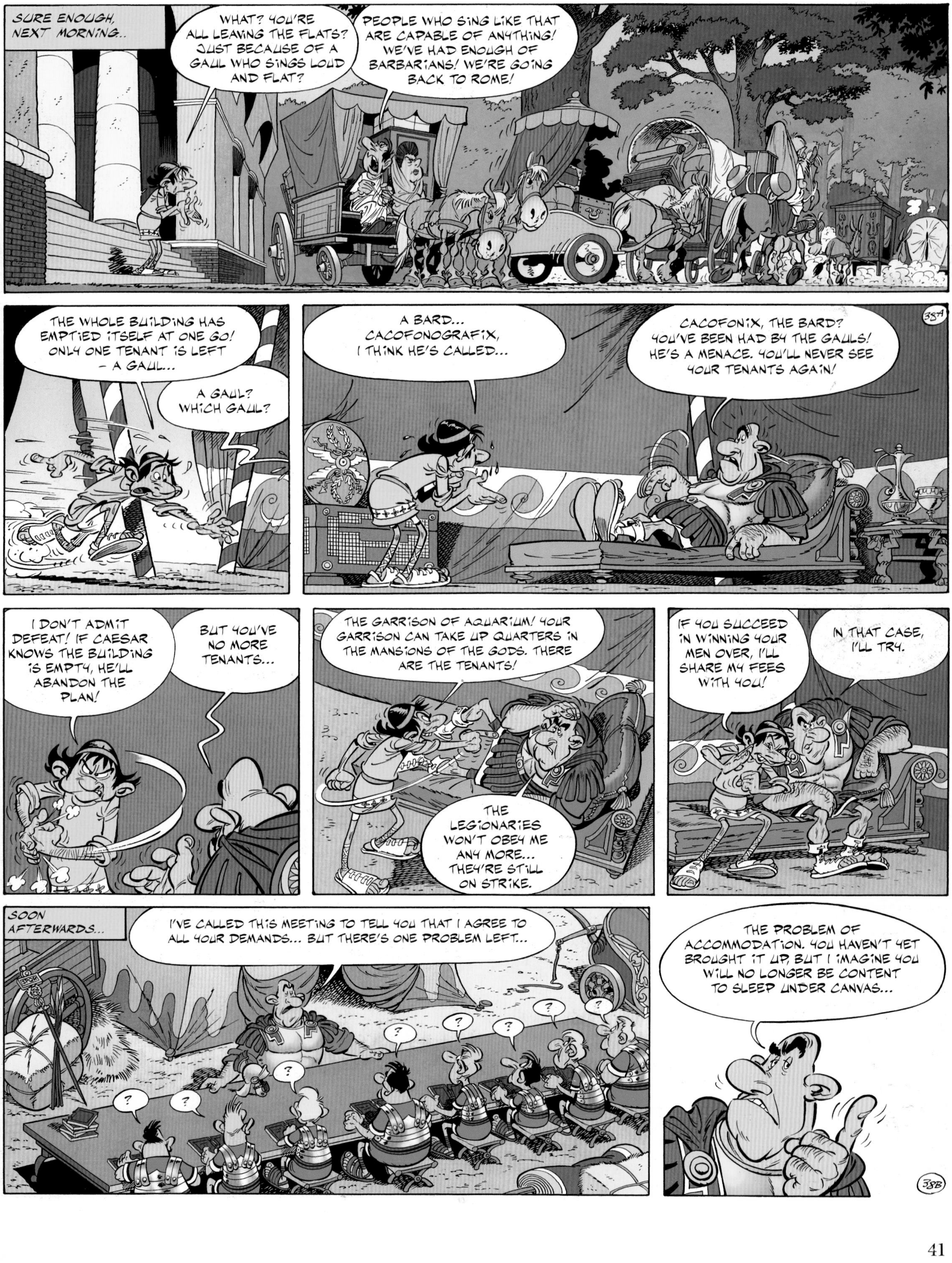

SURE ENOUGH, NEXT MORNING...
WHAT? YOU'RE ALL LEAVING THE FLATS? JUST BECAUSE OF A GAUL WHO SINGS LOUD AND FLAT?
PEOPLE WHO SING LIKE THAT ARE CAPABLE OF ANYTHING! WE'VE HAD ENOUGH OF BARBARIANS! WE'RE GOING BACK TO ROME!
THE WHOLE BUILDING HAS EMPTIED ITSELF AT ONE GO! ONLY ONE TENANT IS LEFT – A GAUL...
A GAUL? WHICH GAUL?
A BARD... CACOFONOGRAFIX, I THINK HE'S CALLED...
38A
CACOFONIX, THE BARD? YOU'VE BEEN HAD BY THE GAULS! HE'S A MENACE. YOU'LL NEVER SEE YOUR TENANTS AGAIN!
I DON'T ADMIT DEFEAT! IF CAESAR KNOWS THE BUILDING IS EMPTY, HE'LL ABANDON THE PLAN!
BUT YOU'VE NO MORE TENANTS...
THE GARRISON OF AQUARIUM! YOUR GARRISON CAN TAKE UP QUARTERS IN THE MANSIONS OF THE GODS. THERE ARE THE TENANTS!
THE LEGIONARIES WON'T OBEY ME ANY MORE... THEY'RE STILL ON STRIKE.
IF YOU SUCCEED IN WINNING YOUR MEN OVER, I'LL SHARE MY FEES WITH YOU!
IN THAT CASE, I'LL TRY.
SOON AFTERWARDS...
I'VE CALLED THIS MEETING TO TELL YOU THAT I AGREE TO ALL YOUR DEMANDS... BUT THERE'S ONE PROBLEM LEFT...
? ? ? ? ? ? ? ? ?
THE PROBLEM OF ACCOMMODATION. YOU HAVEN'T YET BROUGHT IT UP, BUT I IMAGINE YOU WILL NO LONGER BE CONTENT TO SLEEP UNDER CANVAS...
38B

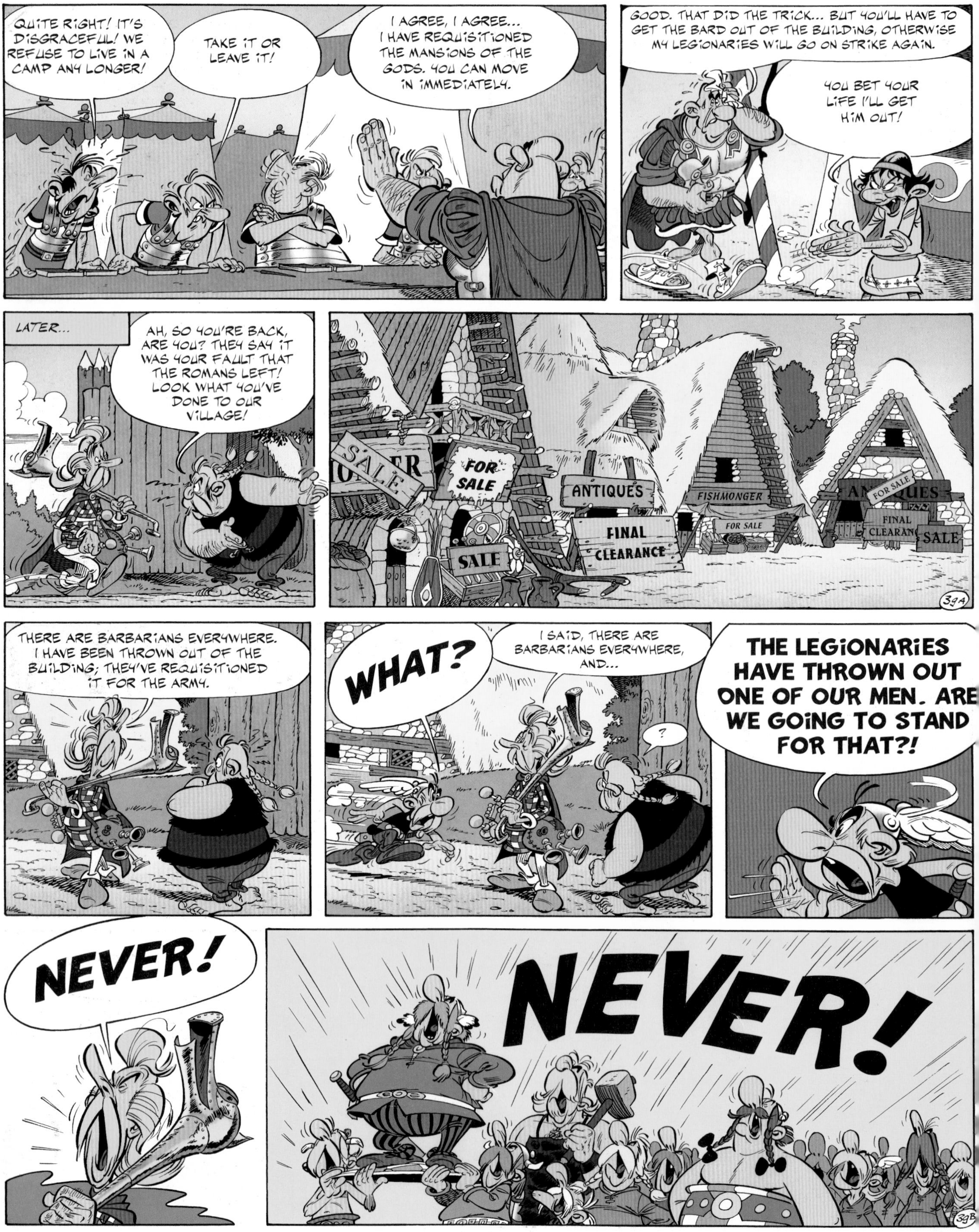
QUITE RIGHT! IT'S DISGRACEFUL! WE REFUSE TO LIVE IN A CAMP ANY LONGER!
TAKE IT OR LEAVE IT!
I AGREE, I AGREE... I HAVE REQUISITIONED THE MANSIONS OF THE GODS. YOU CAN MOVE IN IMMEDIATELY.
GOOD. THAT DID THE TRICK... BUT YOU'LL HAVE TO GET THE BARD OUT OF THE BUILDING, OTHERWISE MY LEGIONARIES WILL GO ON STRIKE AGAIN.
YOU BET YOUR LIFE I'LL GET HIM OUT!
LATER...
AH, SO YOU'RE BACK, ARE YOU? THEY SAY IT WAS YOUR FAULT THAT THE ROMANS LEFT! LOOK WHAT YOU'VE DONE TO OUR VILLAGE!
SALE
FOR SALE
ANTIQUES
FISHMONGER
FOR SALE
FINAL CLEARANCE
SALE
FOR SALE
FINAL
SALE
THERE ARE BARBARIANS EVERYWHERE. I HAVE BEEN THROWN OUT OF THE BUILDING; THEY'VE REQUISITIONED IT FOR THE ARMY.
WHAT?
I SAID, THERE ARE BARBARIANS EVERYWHERE, AND...
?
THE LEGIONARIES HAVE THROWN OUT ONE OF OUR MEN. ARE WE GOING TO STAND FOR THAT?!
NEVER!
NEVER!

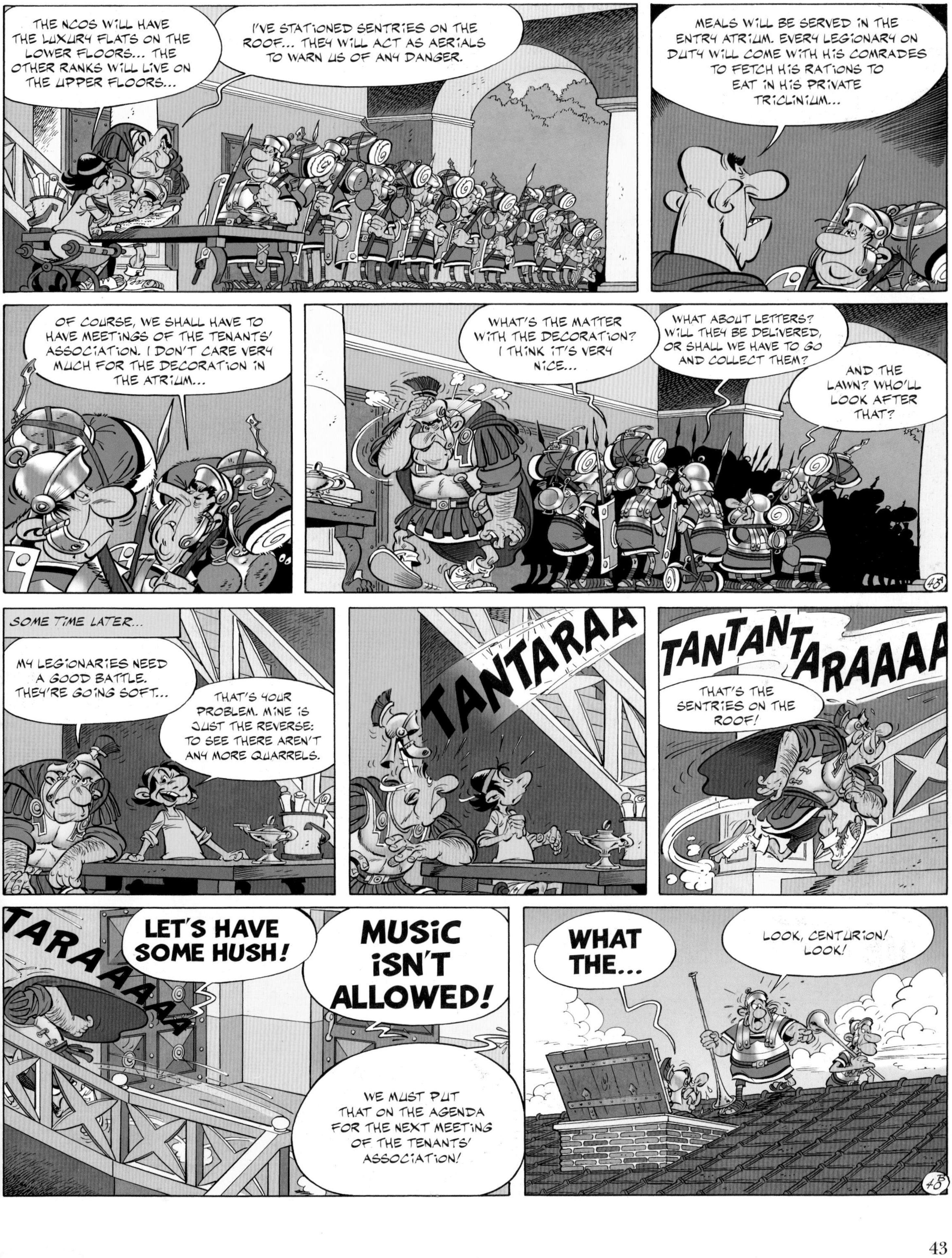
THE NCOS WILL HAVE THE LUXURY FLATS ON THE LOWER FLOORS... THE OTHER RANKS WILL LIVE ON THE UPPER FLOORS...
I'VE STATIONED SENTRIES ON THE ROOF... THEY WILL ACT AS AERIALS TO WARN US OF ANY DANGER.
MEALS WILL BE SERVED IN THE ENTRY ATRIUM. EVERY LEGIONARY ON DUTY WILL COME WITH HIS COMRADES TO FETCH HIS RATIONS TO EAT IN HIS PRIVATE TRICLINIUM...
OF COURSE, WE SHALL HAVE TO HAVE MEETINGS OF THE TENANTS' ASSOCIATION. I DON'T CARE VERY MUCH FOR THE DECORATION IN THE ATRIUM...
WHAT'S THE MATTER WITH THE DECORATION? I THINK IT'S VERY NICE...
WHAT ABOUT LETTERS? WILL THEY BE DELIVERED, OR SHALL WE HAVE TO GO AND COLLECT THEM?
AND THE LAWN? WHO'LL LOOK AFTER THAT?
SOME TIME LATER...
MY LEGIONARIES NEED A GOOD BATTLE. THEY'RE GOING SOFT...
THAT'S YOUR PROBLEM. MINE IS JUST THE REVERSE: TO SEE THERE AREN'T ANY MORE QUARRELS.
TANTARAA
TANTANTARAAAA
THAT'S THE SENTRIES ON THE ROOF!
TARAAAAA
LET'S HAVE SOME HUSH!
MUSIC ISN'T ALLOWED!
WE MUST PUT THAT ON THE AGENDA FOR THE NEXT MEETING OF THE TENANTS' ASSOCIATION!
WHAT THE...
LOOK, CENTURION! LOOK!

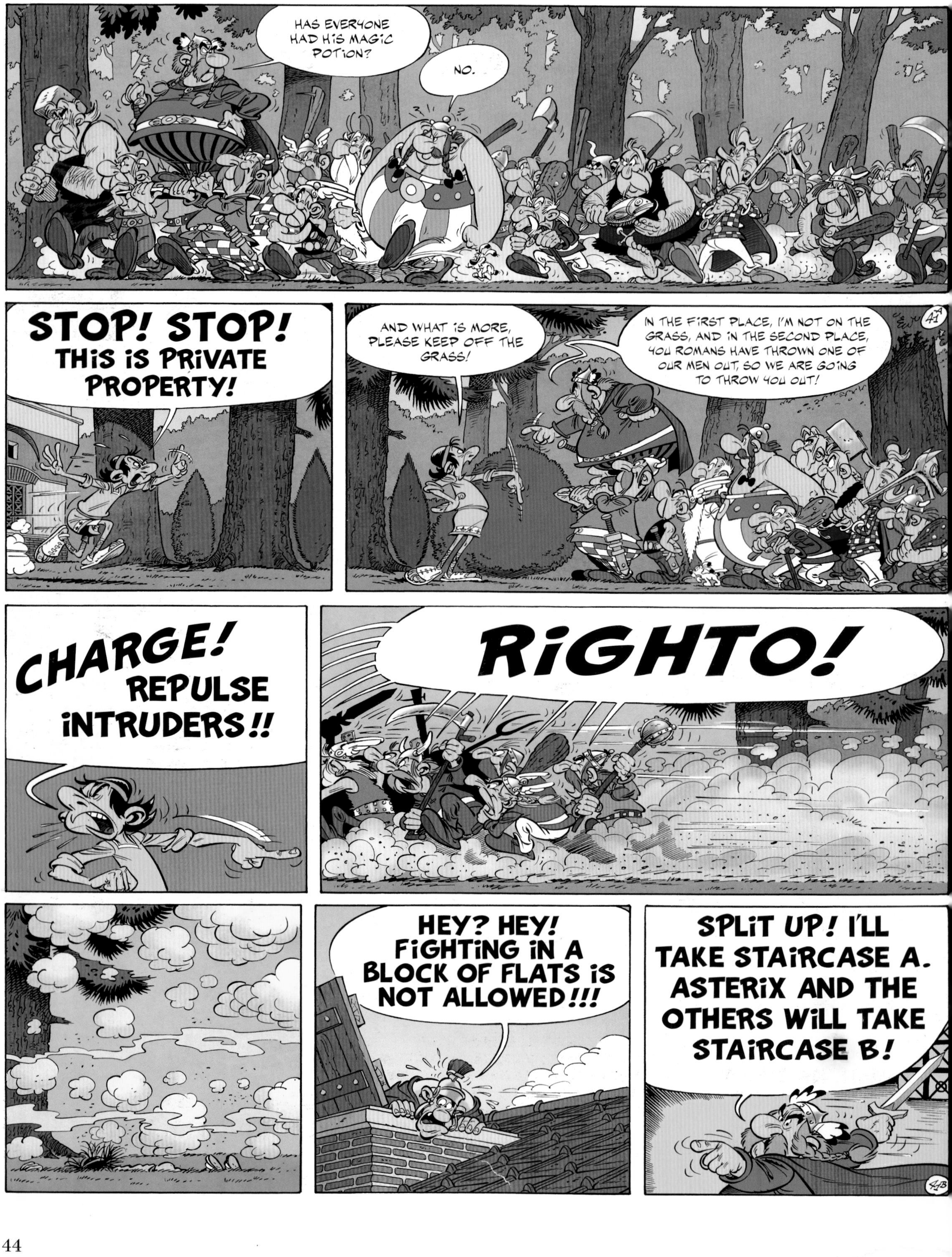

HAS EVERYONE HAD HIS MAGIC POTION?
NO.
STOP! STOP! THIS IS PRIVATE PROPERTY!
AND WHAT IS MORE, PLEASE KEEP OFF THE GRASS!
IN THE FIRST PLACE, I'M NOT ON THE GRASS, AND IN THE SECOND PLACE, YOU ROMANS HAVE THROWN ONE OF OUR MEN OUT, SO WE ARE GOING TO THROW YOU OUT!
CHARGE! REPULSE INTRUDERS!!
RIGHTO!
HEY? HEY! FIGHTING IN A BLOCK OF FLATS IS NOT ALLOWED!!!
SPLIT UP! I'LL TAKE STAIRCASE A. ASTERIX AND THE OTHERS WILL TAKE STAIRCASE B!

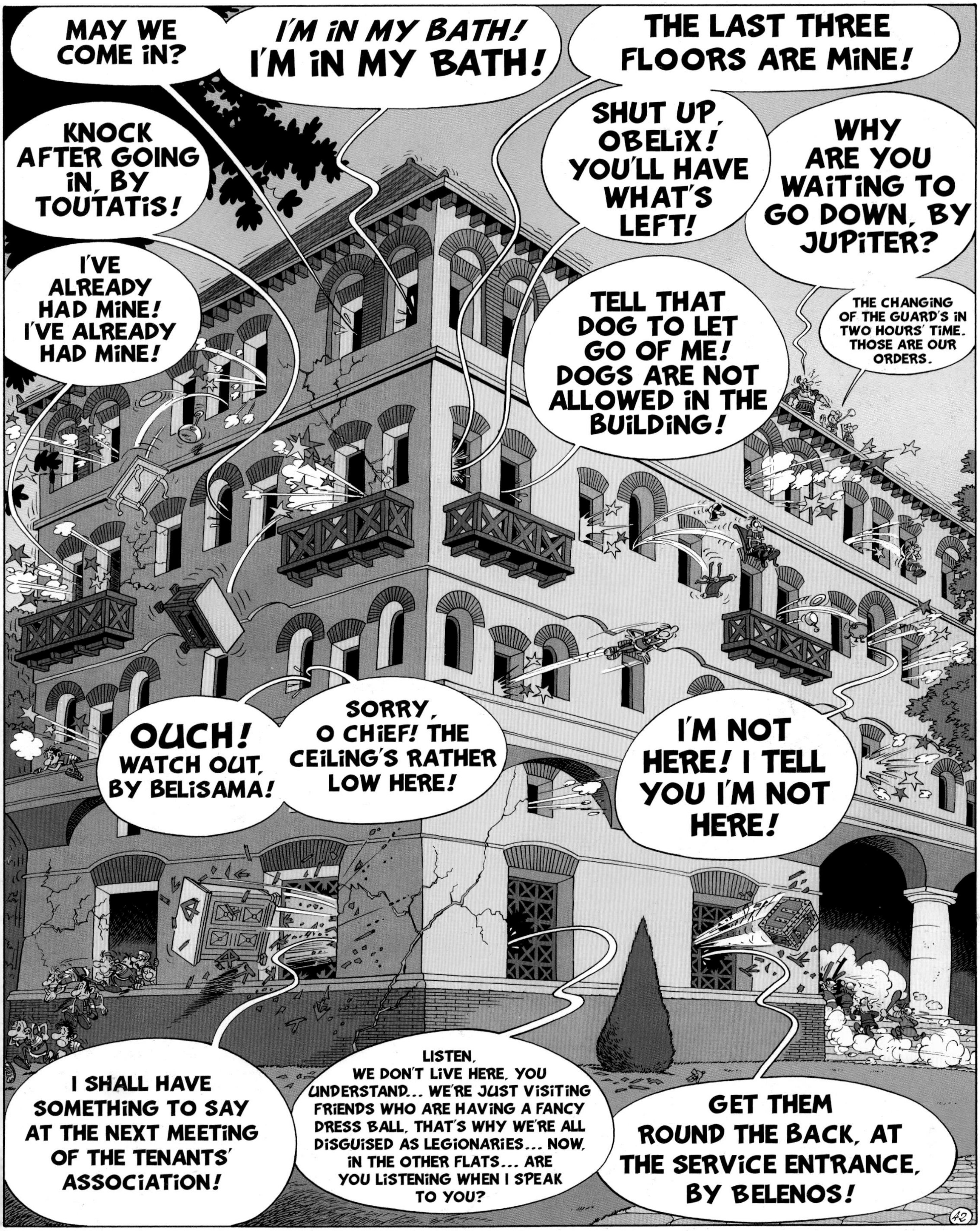

MAY WE COME iN?
I'M iN MY BATH! I'M iN MY BATH!
THE LAST THREE FLOORS ARE MiNE!
KNOCK AFTER GOiNG iN, BY TOUTATiS!
SHUT UP, OBELiX! YOU'LL HAVE WHAT'S LEFT!
WHY ARE YOU WAiTiNG TO GO DOWN, BY JUPiTER?
I'VE ALREADY HAD MiNE! I'VE ALREADY HAD MiNE!
TELL THAT DOG TO LET GO OF ME! DOGS ARE NOT ALLOWED iN THE BUiLDiNG!
THE CHANGiNG OF THE GUARD'S iN TWO HOURS' TiME. THOSE ARE OUR ORDERS.
OUCH! WATCH OUT, BY BELiSAMA!
SORRY, O CHiEF! THE CEiLiNG'S RATHER LOW HERE!
I'M NOT HERE! I TELL YOU I'M NOT HERE!
I SHALL HAVE SOMETHiNG TO SAY AT THE NEXT MEETiNG OF THE TENANTS' ASSOCiATiON!
LiSTEN, WE DON'T LiVE HERE, YOU UNDERSTAND... WE'RE JUST ViSiTiNG FRiENDS WHO ARE HAViNG A FANCY DRESS BALL, THAT'S WHY WE'RE ALL DiSGUiSED AS LEGiONARiES... NOW, iN THE OTHER FLATS... ARE YOU LiSTENiNG WHEN I SPEAK TO YOU?
GET THEM ROUND THE BACK, AT THE SERViCE ENTRANCE, BY BELENOS!
42

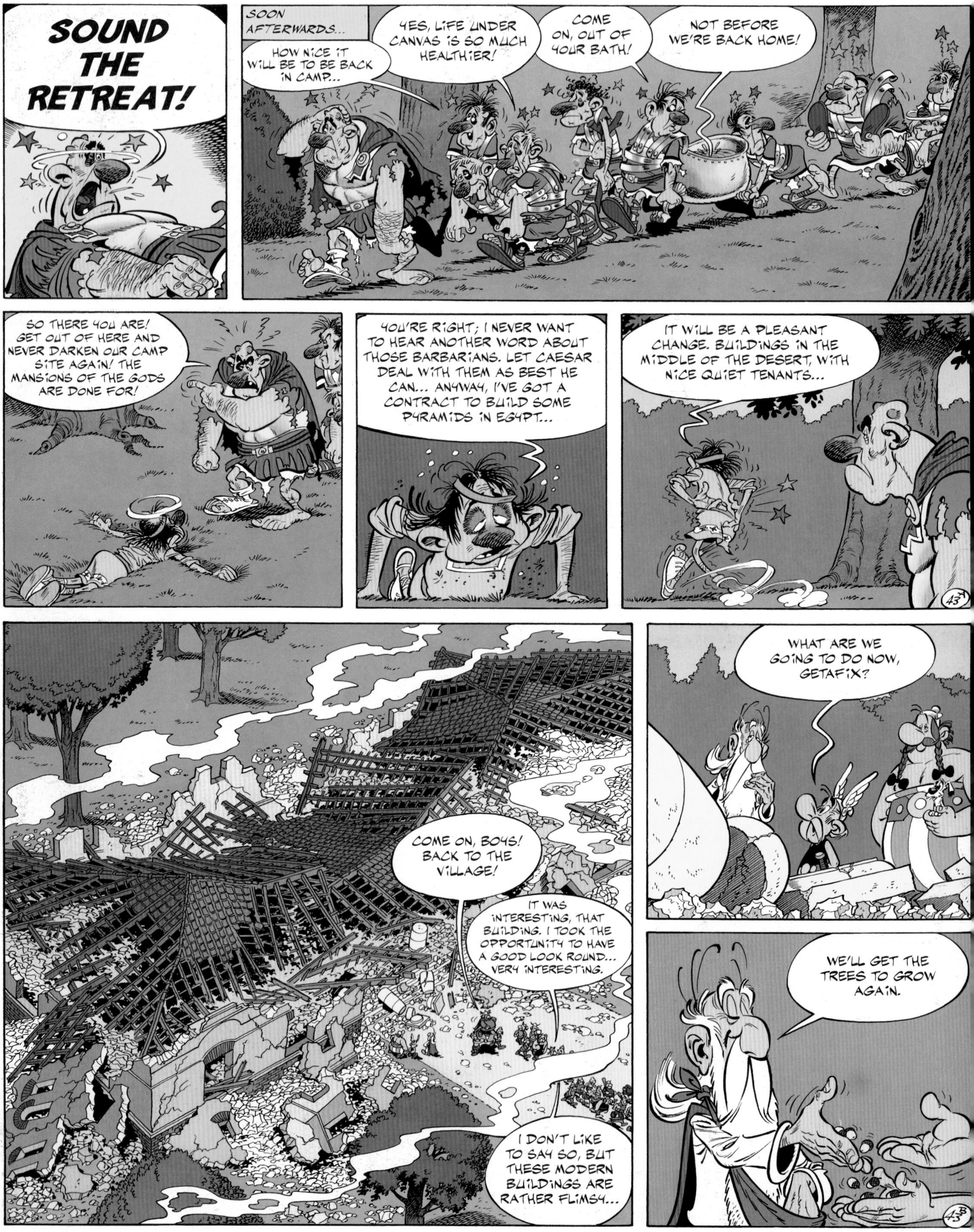
SOUND THE RETREAT!
SOON AFTERWARDS...
HOW NICE IT WILL BE TO BE BACK IN CAMP...
YES, LIFE UNDER CANVAS IS SO MUCH HEALTHIER!
COME ON, OUT OF YOUR BATH!
NOT BEFORE WE'RE BACK HOME!
SO THERE YOU ARE! GET OUT OF HERE AND NEVER DARKEN OUR CAMP SITE AGAIN! THE MANSIONS OF THE GODS ARE DONE FOR!
YOU'RE RIGHT; I NEVER WANT TO HEAR ANOTHER WORD ABOUT THOSE BARBARIANS. LET CAESAR DEAL WITH THEM AS BEST HE CAN... ANYWAY, I'VE GOT A CONTRACT TO BUILD SOME PYRAMIDS IN EGYPT...
IT WILL BE A PLEASANT CHANGE. BUILDINGS IN THE MIDDLE OF THE DESERT, WITH NICE QUIET TENANTS...
COME ON, BOYS! BACK TO THE VILLAGE!
IT WAS INTERESTING, THAT BUILDING. I TOOK THE OPPORTUNITY TO HAVE A GOOD LOOK ROUND... VERY INTERESTING.
I DON'T LIKE TO SAY SO, BUT THESE MODERN BUILDINGS ARE RATHER FLIMSY...
WHAT ARE WE GOING TO DO NOW, GETAFIX?
WE'LL GET THE TREES TO GROW AGAIN.

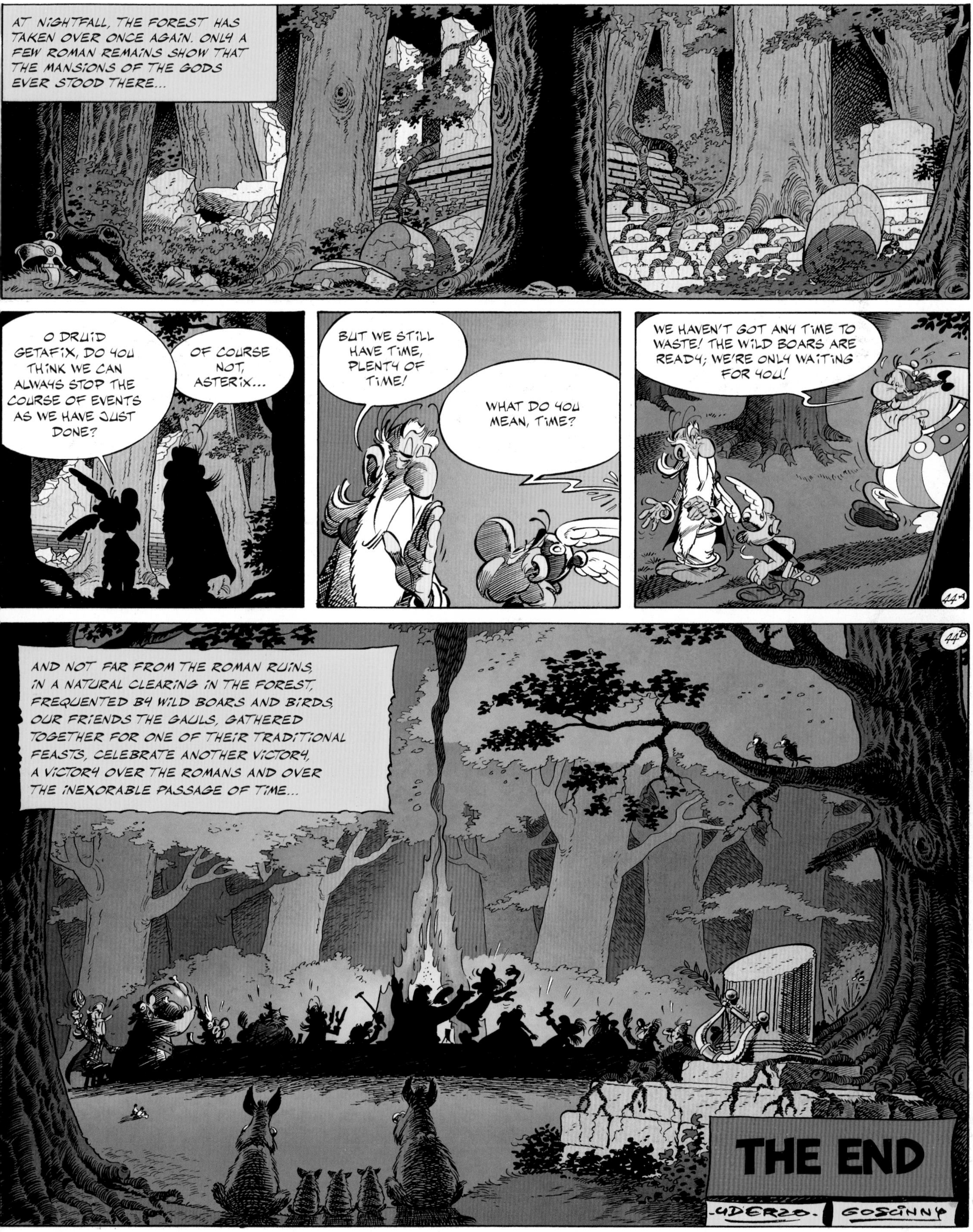

AT NIGHTFALL, THE FOREST HAS TAKEN OVER ONCE AGAIN. ONLY A FEW ROMAN REMAINS SHOW THAT THE MANSIONS OF THE GODS EVER STOOD THERE...
O DRUID GETAFIX, DO YOU THINK WE CAN ALWAYS STOP THE COURSE OF EVENTS AS WE HAVE JUST DONE?
OF COURSE NOT, ASTERIX...
BUT WE STILL HAVE TIME, PLENTY OF TIME!
WHAT DO YOU MEAN, TIME?
WE HAVEN'T GOT ANY TIME TO WASTE! THE WILD BOARS ARE READY; WE'RE ONLY WAITING FOR YOU!
44A
44B
AND NOT FAR FROM THE ROMAN RUINS, IN A NATURAL CLEARING IN THE FOREST, FREQUENTED BY WILD BOARS AND BIRDS, OUR FRIENDS THE GAULS, GATHERED TOGETHER FOR ONE OF THEIR TRADITIONAL FEASTS, CELEBRATE ANOTHER VICTORY, A VICTORY OVER THE ROMANS AND OVER THE INEXORABLE PASSAGE OF TIME...
THE END
UDERZO. GOSCINNY

Asterix titles available now

1 Asterix the Gaul
2 Asterix and the Golden Sickle
3 Asterix and the Goths
4 Asterix the Gladiator
5 Asterix and the Banquet
6 Asterix and Cleopatra
7 Asterix and the Big Fight
8 Asterix in Britain
9 Asterix and the Normans
10 Asterix the Legionary
11 Asterix and the Chieftain's Shield
12 Asterix at the Olympic Games
13 Asterix and the Cauldron
14 Asterix in Spain
15 Asterix and the Roman Agent
16 Asterix in Switzerland
17 The Mansions of the Gods
18 Asterix and the Laurel Wreath
19 Asterix and the Soothsayer
20 Asterix in Corsica
21 Asterix and Caesar's Gift
22 Asterix and the Great Crossing
23 Obelix and Co.
24 Asterix in Belgium
25 Asterix and the Great Divide
26 Asterix and the Black Gold
27 Asterix and Son
28 Asterix and the Magic Carpet
29 Asterix and the Secret Weapon
30 Asterix and Obelix All at Sea
31 Asterix and the Actress
32 Asterix and the Class Act
33 Asterix and the Falling Sky
34 Asterix and Obelix's Birthday – the Golden Book
35 Asterix and the Picts
36 Asterix and the Missing Scroll

Where's Asterix?
Where's Dogmatix?
Asterix and the Vikings
Asterix at the Olympic Games (film tie-in)
How Obelix Fell into the Magic Potion
Asterix Omnibus 1 (Books 1-3)
Asterix Omnibus 2 (Books 4-6)
Asterix Omnibus 3 (Books 7-9)
Asterix Omnibus 4 (Books 10-12)
Asterix Omnibus 5 (Books 13-15)
Asterix Omnibus 6 (Books 16-18)
Asterix Omnibus 7 (Books 19-21)
Asterix Omnibus 8 (Books 22-24)
Asterix Omnibus 9 (Books 25-27)
Asterix Omnibus 10 (Books 28-30)
Asterix Omnibus 11 (Books 31-33)

ORION CHILDREN'S BOOKS

This revised edition first published in 2004 by Orion Books Ltd
This edition published in 2016 by Hodder and Stoughton

15

Original title: *Le Domaine des dieux*

Exclusive licensee: Hachette Children's Group
Translators: Anthea Bell and Derek Hockridge
Typography: Bryony Newhouse

A CIP record for this book is available from the British Library

ISBN 978-0-7528-6638-3 (cased)
ISBN 978-0-7528-6639-0 (paperback)
ISBN 978-1-4440-1324-5 (ebook)

Printed in China
The paper and board used in this book are from well-managed forests and other responsible sources.

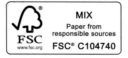

FSC www.fsc.org MIX Paper from responsible sources FSC® C104740

Orion Children's Books
An imprint of Hachette Children's Group, part of Hodder and Stoughton
Carmelite House, 50 Victoria Embankment
London EC4Y 0DZ
An Hachette UK Company

www.hachette.co.uk
www.asterix.com
www.hachettechildrens.co.uk